THE SPIDER:
REIGN OF THE DEATH FIDDLER

THE **MASTER** of **MEN** !

SPIDER®

REIGN OF
THE DEATH FIDDLER

By Grant Stockbridge

STEEGER BOOKS • 2020

CHAPTER 1
BRAND OF DEATH

BRAKES SQUEALED viciously just beside Wentworth and he whirled toward the sound with his cane poised like a sword. A handsome limousine had been crowded to the curb by a smaller sedan. Even as Wentworth watched, three men with guns in their fists boiled out of the sedan and converged on the other car.

Anger swept over Wentworth like a wave. Every night now a score of such robberies were being perpetrated. And he, in three months of effort, had been unable to run to earth the new criminal leader who was responsible—a leader who had bred such a contempt for the law in his followers that they dared to strike within a few hundred feet of Police Headquarters itself—as these men were striking now.

Wentworth cursed under his breath. He was without weapons—his permits having been recently revoked at the insistence of the Mayor—and even now he was on his way to a newly established hideout near the Bowery, where he hoped to obtain a valuable clue to the identity of this new criminal leader.

Yet he could not stand idly by, now. Even as he stepped lithely forward, a bandit's automatic blasted and the chauffeur, who had attempted a defense of the limousine, slumped forward over the steering wheel, his own gun thumping to the floor.

The limousine's one passenger, a woman wrapped in white

1

furs, began to scream—shrill explosive shrieks that hurt the ears. The bandits deployed, one on each side with an eye on the chauffeur while one stepped briskly toward the rear to rob the woman. He had seized the door handle when Wentworth tapped him on the shoulder with his cane.

"Just a minute, my dear fellow." With an effort he masked

Bill Horace blasted away at the Death Fiddler's body!

anger beneath a suave exterior. "I don't believe the young lady wants to make your acquaintance."

The bandit whirled with a snarl, and Wentworth's cane broke his knuckles. The man's automatic dropped to the pavement.

"Thank you," Wentworth said, and stooped for the gun.

The other two bandits had ignored Wentworth's presence—no doubt expecting him to take to his heels at the first threat of violence. His nonchalant interruption took them by surprise. Now, as he felt for the fallen gun—without success—the nearest of the pair threw down on him.

Wentworth caught the coat of the injured crook and jerked him forward off balance—just in time to have him take his companion's bullet in the ribs. Before the gunman could shoot again, Wentworth pulled the head loose from his cane. It separated with a shrill whisper of steel and he came up from his crouch with a rush, the short-bladed sword his cane had concealed burying half its length in the breast of the killer.

The man stood perfectly straight for a count of three. Then his head went back with a strangled cough, and he slumped to the pavement.

Wentworth smiled grimly as he stooped to snatch for the second crook's gun. For Wentworth was the Spider. And to the Spider, champion of oppressed humanity, crusader against crime, there was a joy in any righteous battle for mankind. Even now the fighting blood was singing through his veins.

IF THE man on the other side of the limousine had ideas of staying to fight, the Spider's grim chuckle changed his mind. He took to his heels precipitately as Wentworth, captured gun in hand, leaped clear of the tangle of bodies. But the Spider flung up the gun, came down to sight as calmly as on the target range, and fired twice.

The bullets caught the gunman in the head as he was twisting

4

away. His body spun about and he hit the pavement with his shoulders. His legs flew high, and the momentum of his dash rolled his body over on its face.

Wentworth looked down at the gun in his hand and, weighing it on his palm, nodded. It was a very satisfactory weapon.

He turned toward the limousine. The chauffeur's terrified face was peering whitely at him through the windshield. A dark splotch showed on the man's left shoulder—notwithstanding which he wrenched the car backward suddenly, kept the motor roaring at full speed until it backed around a corner half a block away, then spurted ahead, northward.

Wentworth whipped a silken handkerchief from his breast pocket, polished the automatic clean of fingerprints and tossed it ringingly to the pavement. He caught up his sword, wiped its blade on his victim's clothing, and sheathed it once more in his cane. Then his hand dropped to his vest pocket and came away with a platinum cigarette lighter. Somewhere off to the west a police whistle began burbling frantically, but Wentworth still stood looking down at the bodies.

He was a handsome, lithe figure, with squared, confident shoulders and an arrogant poise to his head. Yet, despite the nonchalance of his stance—as he stood there leaning upon his cane his thin-jawed face was hard and there were cold lights in his gray-blue eyes. He was thinking that, for the healthful example it would impart to the rest of the Underworld, these men should be found with the Spider's scarlet seal upon their foreheads.

Yet he had promised himself never again to use that dread

symbol while in his own identity. It
was too dangerous to him personally
and—a more cogent reason still to
him—his mere identification with
the seal, even if he escaped capture,
would destroy his friend, Stanley
Kirkpatrick, Commissioner of Police.

There were still echoes of the gossip that had followed Kirkpatrick's failure to shoot the Spider when he had had a conspicuous opportunity to do so. Afterward the Spider had shot the
Commissioner through the shoulder. That had settled the gossip
as it had been meant to do—but a very little of the wrong kind
of activity would start all that again.

No, he mustn't do it. That police whistle, too, was piping
nearer now.

But despite his thoughts, Wentworth did not pocket the
cigarette lighter which contained the seals. There were powerful
reasons for imprinting the brand. Since the new Underworld
brain had taken control, criminals had lost all respect and fear
of the law. A series of bold and carefully planned robberies had
been perpetrated; many witnesses had been murdered. A bank
had been looted of half a million, a rich jewelry store stripped.
And the bandits grew increasingly bold.

It was obvious that if the new Underworld leader continued unchecked, the criminal element would soon throw off all
restraint. A major factor in its higher daring was the fact that
no one paid the penalty for any of his crimes. Many had been

arrested, but few had come to trial. And when they did, the witnesses disappeared mysteriously—sometimes even terribly.

It was not the fault of the police. More than twenty of them had been killed lately in pursuit of bandits. But once the criminals escaped from the scene of the crime, they were virtually sure of safety. Thus the morale of the force was breaking.

Wentworth knew the reasons for all this: political protection of the Underworld. There was an unholy alliance of criminals and politicians. That, in fact, was what had blocked him in all his efforts to trace out this new crime leader; that was why, after weeks of failure, he had quit his life of luxury and ease and come to the Underworld to live under the assumed identity of one Limpy Magee, owner and operator of a second-hand shop. That was why, too—for reasons of personal safety—he should not implant his dread seal now.

Personal safety! Wentworth laughed. Slowly, grimly, he stooped above the bodies of the dead. To the paling forehead of each, he pressed his sinister scarlet seal—the emblem of his vengeance—a red spider with sprawled hairy legs and venomous fangs.

He must take this risk in order to strike more surely at that criminal chief. It was time the Underworld felt again the fear of the Spider, merciless killer of the night who wreaked upon them the one vengeance which could chill their blood—the same penalty they meted out to others.

THE SEALS imprinted, Wentworth strode briskly away.

His cane tapped the walk lightly. He moved with a deceptively easy swing, but covered ground rapidly. He could hear the beat of police feet now. The whistling had ended, but that only meant the policeman's call for help had been answered.

Before he had imprinted the seal, Wentworth could have faced down the law. He had killed criminals only—had prevented a holdup. That might have been difficult to prove after the flight of the victims, but probably he could have made it convincing.

Now, however, with the seal of the Spider on the men's foreheads, he would be doomed. He had to get away fast, now. Once let him turn the corner just ahead....

He was hastening toward that corner when around it, with a whistling moan of tires, came a police roadster without lights!

Wentworth jerked his head about. A foot policeman pounded into view behind him. The corner street light glinted on a gun in his hand.

A sharp curse rose in Wentworth's throat. Caught! Surrounded by police. And back there the seal branding him as the Spider already marked his kills!

EVEN AS this flashed through his mind, he was darting away from the police roadster, back toward the lone officer. The cop raced to meet him, shouting as he ran.

"Halt! Halt, or I'll fire!"

His gun belched flame. But the lead screamed overhead as Wentworth ducked. He hurtled into a doorway, ran along the dim hall behind, then crouched beneath the stairs. The policeman's heavy feet pelted toward him. Outside, the patrol car squealed to a halt.

Wentworth's lips were hard against his teeth. He did not fight police. He helped them by rounding up criminals they could not touch. Yet in their eyes the Spider was a wanton murderer! It was not their business to analyze the reasons behind his kills. So they hunted him as furiously as did the Underworld upon which he preyed.

Still, Wentworth could not permit himself to be captured. Even if he escaped later, the delay would ruin all his plans for the night. Already, he might be too late to keep his rendezvous with Danny Dawson, master cracksman.

Not that Danny knew he had a rendezvous with the Spider— or that through him the Spider hoped to gain a clue to the new Underworld chief himself! Danny had merely stated to a friendly barkeep that he wasn't drinking because he had a "job that night." Wentworth, in his disguise as Limpy Magee, had overheard. He planned to trail Danny to the job and thus gain the clue that, during three months of increasing criminal activity, he had failed to find.

PAST THE Spider's hiding place the cop stormed, panting, gun in hand. Wentworth's cane licked out. The rubber-tipped ferrule caught the policeman behind the ear and spilled him heavily to the floor. His gun skated along the hall, bumped the wall, and discharged with a slamming roar.

The two policemen from the car had plunged into the doorway, but with the shot they ducked to cover. And while they did so, Wentworth ran on soundless feet to the back door, and out into the protective darkness of the night.

Five minutes later, after threading a devious way among debris-piled yards and across two empty streets, he entered a back entrance to the basement of a slatternly frame house.

In the darkness he threw on the light of a pocket flash. It showed the way to a brick which, as he pressed it, opened a door in the apparently solid foundation wall. He stepped inside, and minutes later an entirely different figure emerged. Wentworth was now Limpy Magee, owner of the second-hand shop beneath which he had effected this transformation.

His left leg held stiff by a contrivance of steel and rubber-padded straps, he limped heavily up the cellar steps. His shoulders were slouched, his hair was a tousled, mouse-colored mop above a lumpy, grimed forehead.

He had scarcely stumped into the shop and unlocked the door when a policeman with a drawn gun stalked belligerently into his shop.

"I'm frisking this dump," he said harshly.

"What d'yah want me to do, cheer about it?" snarled Limpy Magee, alias Wentworth.

When the cop had searched the shop, the cellar, even the living quarters above a narrow flight of creaking stairs—and found nothing—he confronted Wentworth once more in the cluttered store. Other police were marching by in patrols, entering every doorway and vacant lot.

"What's the big idea?" Wentworth demanded. "A kid been snatched?"

The cop grinned crookedly. "Better wash your forehead, Limpy. The Spider's somewhere around this block. Maybe he's coming to stick a seal on you."

Wentworth began to curse in the best Limpy Magee manner. He shook his clenched fists over his head at the jeering policeman and, when the officer was gone, stumped about in angry circles. But inwardly he was chuckling. The cop's warning gave him a good reason for leaving his shop. And in a very few minutes now he must be ready to follow Danny Dawson when Danny went on his "job."

LIMPY MAGEE

Hobbling to the door, Wentworth shouted across the street. Presently a thin, worn girl of twenty or so came to the shop. She was shivering beneath the thin shawl which was her only wrap.

"You want me, Mr. Magee?" she asked timidly.

"What d'yah suppose I called you for?" he asked gruffly. "Keep shop till I come back."

The girl smiled up at him. "Yes, Mr. Magee."

His gruffness did not frighten her. He paid her well for keeping the shop during his many absences. Much too well, in fact.

Hastily Wentworth limped out and up the street. His lumpy forehead was hidden under a greasy cap, his unpressed suit lay like a bag about him. He was lucky: Danny was just leaving his own frowsy quarters and walking furtively up the street. Inconspicuously, Wentworth trailed him in a battered old coupé he had stolen for the night's work. He would pay the owner well....

THE SPIDER had no trouble in following Danny to the house he intended burglarizing. A few minutes after the yegg entered, Wentworth put in a call for police. Then he went in

11

behind Danny. He found the cracksman, frightened but venomous, behind a leveled gun, ready to kill.

"Cheez... wait!" Wentworth exploded the words in a scared whisper, and was going on to explain how he had just happened to try for the same jewels this same night—when a police siren sounded.

"God, let's get outa here!" he cried then. They fled, together, out to the stolen coupé.

Once in it and moving, however, its motor proved feeble. Police guns were still banging behind as they neared the vicinity of their respective hangouts on the Bowery.

Danny Dawson was terrified. "We're gone," he whined. "Oh God, we're caught!"

Wentworth crouched lower over the wheel, tried to jockey another half mile of speed out of the bellowing motor. He laughed softly. To the Spider this night was well worth its risks if, through it, he gained Danny's confidence, or a clue to this newly arisen master of crime....

Danny screamed as a bullet smashed the rear window of the coupé, stinging his neck with flying fragments. Wentworth crouched still lower and, narrow-eyed and tense, peered along the night-darkened street.

Black steel pillars of the elevated railway threw shadows across the path. Close walls flung back the racket of the motors and banging guns. If the police would just keep on missing for three blocks more....

A hissing blast rocked the coupé. A rear tire had been shot off. The car veered wildly, raced head-on for a steel elevated pillar. Wentworth threw all his weight into a wrench upon the steering wheel. The coupé lifted on two wheels, wavered, then bounced off the pillar, skated into the left-  hand lane of traffic. For frantic moments, Wentworth fought to prevent the car from capsizing. Then he reached a corner and yawed around it.

"Get ready to jump, Danny!" he shouted. "We've got to...."

The coupé rammed against a lamp post, and steam jetted from the radiator. The windshield collapsed inward. Flinging out to the street Wentworth plunged head down for the black mouth of an alley farther along the block.

The race was no longer on even terms. Police could easily overtake men on foot. Yet Wentworth's laughter lingered on his lips in a stiff smile.

If he and Danny both came through this, he would have Danny's confidence all right, perhaps a clue to the Underworld chief! Damn this artificially stiff leg. It hampered his movements....

A screech of skidding tires swept his mind clean of all thought except escape. The police car had rocketed around the corner behind them. Guns spoke eagerly.

"The alley, Danny!" Wentworth yelled. "Duck into the alley!"

Danny was zig-zagging down the pavement, frantic shrieks jerking from his lips. He was within twenty feet of the alley's safety when, with a shrill bleat of terror, he flopped crashingly upon his face.

CHAPTER 2
THE MASTER'S WARNING

WENTWORTH CURSED as he raced to Danny's side and dragged him toward the alley. Bullets whined closer now, and despair gripped him. He had risked much to win the confidence of the safecracker, only to have a police bullet....

Well, he would play his cards to the limit. He knew this territory as only a man who must be alert for assassins at every breath could know it.

Lead clipped the bricks inches away from his head as be dragged Danny into the alley. He dropped to the ground, wriggled through a warehouse window, still dragging the other after him. He shouldered the unconscious yegg, groped across the basement. The gray light of another window showed on the opposite side. Through that he crawled, and into a dark street, where he moved in a jolting trot with his burden. Reaching a dark doorway a hundred feet up another alley, pounded on it insistently. Three knocks—two knocks—three knocks.

Often, crouched in this dark alley, he had heard the signal for admittance to Collins' back room. He knew the place was barred to all save the criminally elite—Danny Dawson being among them. Here, if anywhere, he could get information about the chief of the Underworld... And even dead, Danny could help him, could gain Limpy Magee an entrance here.

A slot in the door opened and a beam of light slid out. Wentworth held Danny so that the light hit the cracksman's face.

"Quick! It's Danny Dawson!" he gasped. "A cop drilled him!"

The door jerked open and Wentworth staggered in with his burden. He was led rapidly up a steep flight of stairs, into a room where he was able to lay Danny down on a cot and look at him. And then his eyes brightened with joy. The wound was only a crease across the scalp.

It took fifteen minutes to revive Danny, during which time Wentworth was helped by three obviously hostile men. Danny finally looked up with a sickly grin and held out a shaking slender hand.

"You're a pal, Limpy Magee," he said weakly. "I was a goner and you snatched me out of it."

As he told the three hard faced hoods what had happened, their hostility faded.

"I vouch for Limpy, see," Danny told them "He's my pard." A half hour later he was feeling well enough to lead Wentworth downstairs into the crowded back room of Collins' saloon.

IT WAS a ratty little place with smoke-greased walls, shut off from a bar to the front by a wooden partition. Round wooden tables were jammed into it, with men and women crowded about them. Against the street wall was a tiny cleared space for dancing, partly occupied by a piano which, as Wentworth entered, was being thumped tinnily by a thin man who wore a derby.

The story of his rescue of Danny had gone before, so that men and women, whose faces adorned the rogue's galleries of half the continent, greeted him as Limpy Magee with easy familiarity.

A dark girl in a tight red dress jumped up and squeezed his rock-hard biceps.

"Think you could carry *me*, Limpy?" she cooed.

Wentworth caught her by the waist and hoisted her to a seat on his left shoulder. Her heels drummed his chest and, laughing he snatched a neat automatic from a garter holster inside her right knee.

"Damn you, Limpy!" She twisted both hands into his mouse-colored hair and he set her down quickly lest she pull off his wig.

The girl snatched back her gun and, for a moment, seemed on the point of shoot-

Wentworth's hand flashed across
his chest and snatched out a
blue-gleaming automatic!

ing him. Then she laughed, caught his ears with both hands, kissed him, and swaggered back to her seat.

A pretty little creature, Wentworth thought to himself. But he had instantly identified her. She was suspected of having shot two men to death in a jewelry store holdup. Snakey Annie, they called her. She had that kind of eyes.

Her gesture to Wentworth was the final accolade of the Underworld. From now on, Limpy Magee belonged. He limped heavily, on his stiff leg, toward a table. Contemptuously Danny palmed a lesser crook from a chair and a broad-beamed waiter slopped liquor between them.

"You're a pal, Limpy," said Danny lifting his glass. "Here's to you."

They tossed that one off and Wentworth let his eyes stray slowly over the tobacco fogged room. The place was rife with the odor of stale beer and whisky, and under-washed humanity.

He saw that Snakey Annie was glowering at him over her whisky glass. She pushed to her feet and began to weave her way toward him. Danny laughed softly, a shrill whinny.

"It's just too bad if you've got another goil, Limpy," he said. "Snakey Annie's got her eye on ya."

Wentworth grunted disdainfully as he inspected others in the rowdy, dangerous crowd. He was an unprepossessing figure in Limpy Magee's greasy, unpressed suit. The mouse-colored hair sprawled across a lumpy forehead and a two-day beard glistened on his jowls. With a bulbous nose and hard eyes squeezed by wrinkled flesh, Limpy Magee looked to be a dour, disgruntled fellow of forty-odd. His second-hand shop on Clancy was a good "front" where, it was whispered, he had been known to buy up plenty of stolen jewelry.

But even though the Underworld had heard this, even though his supposed Chicago background had been carefully synthesized, he had arrived too recently to be fully trusted.

Snakey Annie dropped into a seat across the table and Wentworth resolutely kept his eyes scanning the room. Quite aside from the fact that all his love was given to a woman of his own cultured, well-to-do class—Nita van Sloan—he wanted no entanglements with Underworld women. Women were dangerous, in such roles as he played.

AS HE glanced about, a hush dropped over the room. Hoarse laughter died and the tinny piano fell quiet with a discordant crash which lingered as if uneasily in the thick air.

It was a moment before Wentworth found the reason. Then he saw a man, a newcomer, standing at the foot of the steep stairs which slanted across the back part of the room. The man had a fine sweep of white hair across a high forehead, a thin, severe nose upon which pince-nez glasses sat firmly.

But it was not that which opened the loose-lipped mouth of Limpy Magee in a gasp. Across the formal white bosom of the man's dress shirt was a stitching of bullet holes, and from them thin streams of red had trickled. There were four bullet holes in the man's chest, and yet he stood there smiling, nodding to the crooks crowded into the room!

It was Snakey Annie who first recovered from the shock of surprise that gripped the room.

"Nerts," she said, "that guy makes me sick."

Wentworth met the glittering gaze of the girl. "What is that?"

"It's the big cheese, the chief high mucky-de-muck," Annie sneered, twisting her full lips, "He's the boy who's running things these days."

And then Wentworth gulped for another reason. "Cheez!" he cried. "That's Judge Scott! The guy who's so honest he held a cop-killer last week even when he was told he'd get the finger put on him for it!"

Annie laughed throatily. "Naw, that's not the Judge. That's just this guy's way of bragging. He's fixed himself up this way so's to tell the world he's going to murder Judge Scott tonight."

Wentworth looked back to the man again. So this was the new leader, the man he had hunted for weeks to kill!

His fingers ached for the automatic nestling under his left arm. With one shot, he could destroy this man. It was even possible that in the excitement he himself could escape.

But he made no move to draw. After all, this was only the first move in a major battle. He had at last won a chance to come in contact with the Underworld's new chief. But he knew nothing of the other's organization, nothing of how he ruled the criminals and controlled the politicians of the city.

Wentworth had learned one thing. The man had intelligence, a gift for sardonic humor, and a real feeling for the dramatic. Easy to see as much in his present gesture of parading in the garb of the man he intended to kill. He had even indicated how the victim would die!

"He done this for twelve weeks," Danny Dawson whispered admiringly, "and he's called the turn every time."

For twelve weeks. Yes, there had been that many murders. Every Thursday night at eleven thirty—it was as if this criminal master scorned anything so obvious as a midnight murder—a man or woman had been killed. Rarely was it the same means of death, or the same class of person. A crook had been tossed from a window; a woman clubbed; a millionaire strangled in his sleep. And tonight—Judge Scott was to be shot to death.

WENTWORTH'S MUSCLES jerked as he realized that this was undoubtedly retribution for the judge's refusal this day to dismiss a criminal charged with the murder of a policeman. It was the first time it had been possible to make an arrest stick. The police force, even the business organizations of the city, were becoming demoralized. Since there had been no retribution for crimes, bandits were running wild. There was a score of holdups a day... Judge Scott's action had promised improvement, and now the Underworld chief would remove him.

Wentworth calculated swiftly. It was now about ten o'clock. In an hour and a half Judge Scott would be murdered—unless he could be given warning. Yet, Wentworth knew, he himself hadn't a chance of leaving. Danny would cling to him for hours yet. And Snakey Annie....

A heavy slip on the swinging doors which led to the bar room jerked Wentworth's eyes that way. Then he stiffened in his chair.

A policeman had entered Collins' back room.

Swift thoughts raced through Wentworth's mind. Had the policeman traced him and Danny here? A slow chill crept over his arms—not of fear, but of apprehension. Blood drops might well have left a trail. His own artificially stiff leg made him easily identifiable....

The policeman looked slowly over the foggy room. When his eyes reached Wentworth, they stopped.

Wentworth's muscles were tight and hard, but he returned the policeman's gaze with excellently assumed indifference, his face wrinkled in frowning hostility. He knew that Danny's hand had dropped to a gun. He saw too that Snakey Annie's left hand hovered close to the hem of her skirt, where her automatic was hidden. Blood throbbed in Wentworth's temples and he swallowed, slowly.

Whether or not the policeman had come for him, this officer was doomed. He would see the man in the garb of Judge Scott....

Murder was in the silent tenseness of the room, in the glittering eyes of the criminals. Wentworth realized the policeman's doom and he realized something else: the Spider could do nothing to prevent it. If he moved to protect the policeman, even to warn him of what threatened, all Limpy Magee's hard-won prestige would be wiped out.

Damn the young fool, Wentworth thought, let him die! One life was less important than the capture of the Underworld chief and the smashing of his machine—less important than the preservation of his own identity as Limpy Magee.

The policeman started as his eyes caught sight of the blood-smeared figure across the room. But as the false Judge Scott strolled casually toward him, he apparently did not recognize the imposture; merely suspected some trick.

A barrel-chested bouncer, matted hair curling from the open neck of his shirt, halted before the officer, glowering.

"Git out," he ordered contemptuously.

The cop's straight lips lifted a little at the corners.

"Polite to strangers, aren't you?" He pushed past the bouncer, toward a table where a man and a blonde girl sat with heads close together, watching him.

WENTWORTH'S EYES followed, and he felt the throbbing, silent menace of the room. Every face was turned intently toward the man in blue and brass; every face showed lip-licking eagerness for the kill.

The bouncer stood glowering as the policeman bent and spoke in an undertone to the two at the table. One of them, the girl, jumped to her feet the next instant and her chair caromed against an adjacent table.

"I'll do what I damned well please," she cried shrilly.

The man with her got to his feet more slowly. He was small and dark, younger than the policeman.

"I think you'd better get out," he said heavily.

Wentworth made his sly, Limpy Magee features look as eager as any when he saw the bouncer reinforced by two dirty-aproned waiters. They blocked the door. At any moment, from the fog of tobacco smoke, might come the shot that would spill the young policeman dying to the floor.

The cop straightened, meeting the eyes of the two at the table, the slight smile still twisting his lips. He glanced about the room, and for the first time seemed to become aware of his danger. The smile tightened on his lips, but the stick continued to twirl in his hand.

A bitter smile twisted Wentworth's own lips. That officer might be foolhardy, but he had courage. He knew suddenly that, regardless of the peril to himself and to his efforts to trap the Underworld leader he could not stand by and see crooks butcher this fine young officer. The Spider would have to go to his defense.

Wentworth tossed off his drink, leaned across the table toward Danny.

"Watch me have some fun with the copper," he whispered.

Danny's eyes widened, but Wentworth shoved back his chair and a score of heads swung his way. Snakey Annie started to her feet, eyes glistening in admiration. Wentworth swaggered with his stiff-legged limp toward the doomed policeman.

"Stand back," the cop ordered quietly.

"Aw, don't get sore," Wentworth smirked. His voice insolent, he kept limping forward.

Jeering laughter rippled over the room. Wentworth was already a hero and his swaggering pleased them. Wentworth's blue-gray gaze locked with that of the policeman, whose indignant face was slightly flushed. His wide shoulders were braced and he carried his head with a certain erect pride.

Wentworth walked up close and poked out his chin: "Did you say something to me?" he demanded.

THE POLICEMAN put a hand in Wentworth's face and shoved him back two paces. Jeering laughter started—and stopped as Wentworth's hand flashed across his chest and snatched out a shining blue automatic. The policeman's mouth opened, color drained from his face. He pawed frantically beneath the tail of his coat.

Wentworth heard a cry he guessed came from the gang leader. He laughed shortly and fired. The policeman's cap was bullet-jolted from his forehead, which was divided by a streak of blood. Then his head sagged, his knees hit the floor and he pitched forward on his face.

Wentworth nodded slowly. Deliberately he thumbed on the safety of his automatic before he thrust it back into the holster. He turned toward the crowd and grinned slowly.

"Sorry to steal all the fun," he said thickly. "I don't like cops should push me in the face."

There was a moment of stunned silence, then a burst of violent laughter. The Underworld leader with his falsely blooded breast looked at Wentworth with still eyes.

"Hot stuff, Limpy!" a man yelled. "You're all right."

The small dark man to whom the policeman had spoken snarled a curse. His face was suffused with anger. He caught up a bottle and flung it at Wentworth's head, then rushed in after it. Behind him, the blonde girl stood stiffly, staring at the policeman on the floor. Wentworth caught the bottle in mid-air and smacked its base on the man's head. The gangster crumpled, his face striking Wentworth's shoes.

The girl screamed and went around the table, toward the policeman. Wentworth stepped into her path, caught her by the arm, jerked her close to his sneering disguised face.

"Wait a minute, honey," he drawled, "just what are you aimin' to do?"

The girl pummeled at his face with her fists and Wentworth yanked her wrists down behind her, pulled her closer, so that he looked down into large, panic-stricken blue eyes. Her tip-tilted hat had slid off and hair like spun silver cascaded over her shoulders.

"You beast!" she sobbed. "You *beast!* You killed Billy and now you've killed Jerry. You wait…."

Wentworth lifted a puzzled face and shook his head at the grinning crowd.

"What the hell is it all about?" he asked in bewilderment. "I kill a cop and a guy and a dame get sore at me!"

The girl went limp in Wentworth's arms and he eased her into a chair, then stumbled as something hard thumped behind his ear. He whirled in a crouch and stared into the furious eyes of Snakey Annie.

"You keep your hands off that girl, see," she said, her voice low and hard. "I'm not going to stand for any two-timing…."

Wentworth's eyes widened in amazement, then tightened in simulated anger. Danny Dawson hadn't exaggerated. Snakey Annie had chosen him for her own and because he had wrestled with the other girl… Wentworth stepped forward sharply, twisted away the gun with which she had hit him and slapped her face—hard.

"Listen, baby," he said roughly, "I pick my own women, see? Now layoff before you get hurt."

Snakey Annie was sucking in dry sobbing breaths. There were no tears in her eyes, but her gaze was bewildered.

Wentworth's blood was singing in his veins. Now he could warn the police to guard Judge Scott. He could return and follow the Underworld chief in his macabre disguise when he left. He looked sharply about the room... The gang chief had vanished!

CHAPTER 3
THE GANG CHIEF'S TRIUMPH

WENTWORTH CHOKED down a curse; whirled toward the swing doors that opened to the front. Even now, he could have overtaken the chief—except for this policeman at his feet. He still had to carry the young fool from the saloon, to safety....

A heavy hand topped each half of the swing doors and they folded in to show a squat, heavy-set man with harsh black hair and a bearded face. He frowned down at the policeman, and the bouncer gave a hurried explanation. Wentworth knew the man. It was Collins, owner of the saloon.

"That's okay," Collins said in a surprisingly light, thin voice, "but Limpy will have to get the corpse out of here. I don't mind a bit of good clean fun, but...."

A gust of laughter swept the room and Wentworth grinned. "Okay," he said. "I'll get him out."

He went down on a knee, pulled the cop's arms across his shoulders, gruntingly heaved the man up in fireman's lift. As he

stood with the blue-coated figure curled across his shoulders, the bouncer peered at him with bulging eyes.

"Cheez, Limpy," he gulped. "I never knew youse had it in ya."

Wentworth still frowned. "You don't know nothing," he grunted at the bouncer. "Open them doors."

The barrel-chested bouncer hopped to hold open the doors and Wentworth limped out through the front room where two bartenders stared in amazement. Danny came after him, but Wentworth drove him back.

"I'll see you after I get rid of this."

It was a monstrous commentary of the crime wave bred by the new chief, that the Bowery was virtually deserted and that no policeman had come to investigate the shot. Wentworth shouldered the cop into a battered old sedan at the curb—Limpy Magee's own car, which he had parked there earlier in the day for use in switching cars after his escape from the police with Danny—and drove off while a crowd watched open-mouthed from the doorway.

A pleasant smile was on Wentworth's lips when, after stopping long enough to phone Commissioner Kirkpatrick from a corner drug store, he stopped before his shop in Clancy Street. He had rescued the policeman from certain death and got away in time to phone the warning about Judge Scott. By now police guards would be thrown about the judge's home. Moreover, if he had not been able to follow the Underworld leader, he had at least performed an exploit which would attract the man's further attention.

Unlocking the door of his shop with its dust-smeared glass panel, he carried the policemen through a clutter of second-hand stuff up the creaking flight of stairs. On the second floor, he handcuffed the other to the bed, and began bathing the wound on his forehead.

THAT SHOT had been dangerous. It had been necessary to aim at precisely the right angle, or the glancing bullet which creased the policeman's skull might very well have broken the bone.

The policeman regained consciousness with a groan and a toss of his head. It was several minutes before he could glare up at Wentworth with pain-filled eyes.

"Listen, guy," he said harshly, "you turn me loose damned quick"

Wentworth nodded mildly. "Okay. But listen, ya wanta know why I did what I did? Well, I hated to see a young cop killed. So I took this way of snatching you out of bigger danger, see?"

The cop glared his unbelief. "Baloney," he snarled.

Wentworth shrugged. "Then figger out why I didn't drill you through the belly, and why I missed up close like that.

"Look," said Wentworth, still in the role of Limpy Magee. "I want to show you sump'n." He walked across the room to the wall, twenty feet away and set three dimes on their edges on the top of a table against the wall. Then he returned to the policeman's bedside and snapped out his automatic. He fired three times, and where the dimes had been were three holes in the wall. The top of the table was not scarred.

The policeman's face was white with something besides pain. "That was shooting," he said slowly.

Wentworth nodded dourly at the man's forehead. "So was that, if you asks me. Now listen. I want some dope from you. I found out from some letters that you're William R. Horace of the Clinton Street precinct. But who was the guy and the dame you was talking to?"

The policeman closed his eyes as if they hurt him and talked that way. "I owe you considerable for not killing me back there in Collins'," he said slowly. "The man was my brother, Jerry, and the girl was Tony Musette who Jerry's engaged to. Jerry's kind of foolish—" he opened his eyes, looked up earnestly—"but he's not really wild. He deals faro for Big Mike Gallagan and thinks he's tough. He took Tony to Collins' to show off, and I was just telling him it was not a good idea."

Wentworth's lips curved. "You walked into Collins' to tell him it wasn't a good idea, huh?"

The policeman smiled back. "Crooks are yellow," he said firmly.

"Not with forty-to-one odds behind 'em, they ain't," Wentworth corrected. "Now listen. You're going to kick, but I got to leave you here for an hour. Promise not to yell and I won't gag you. I'll turn you loose when I gets back"

"Okay, Limpy," Patrolman Bill Horace agreed. "There's a lot about this that I don't get, but I guess I still owe you something. I won't yell."

IT WAS a vastly different figure than Limpy Magee's which emerged presently from Limpy's shop, to move carefully through the debris-heaped yards to a side street, there to stride off energetically. In body and carriage, the figure was once more Richard Wentworth, clad in the perfectly tailored dark tweeds that suited him so well, a brown Borsalino jauntily across his brows, came swinging. He still, however, wore a wig, and certain disguising things had been done to his face.

He stiffened abruptly, halted in his walk. From ahead came the sounds of raucous laughter and an old woman's shrill protests. Figures wove in and out darkly against a distant street light. Wentworth quickened his pace, jaw tightening. This was part of the wholesale criminality that had been running rampant in the city. An unescorted woman was not safe on the streets after dark.

As he came closer he saw that the woman had a shawl about her head and had backed up against the wall of a building while a half dozen young toughs bedeviled her. They had already dumped her peddler's basket on the street.

"Aw, cut her throat," one growled, "she's making too much noise."

A knife gleamed in the man's hand. Wentworth tapped him on the shoulder.

"Let me have a light, will you please?" he asked gently.

The young tough whirled, the knife held low to strike. Wentworth smiled at him and indicated again the cigarette between his lips. His cane was held lightly in his left hand, its ferrule clear of the pavement and pointed slightly forward.

He was conscious that two of the men were sidling away to encircle him. The old woman, forgotten, braced her shoulders against the wall and waited. She was bent far forward.

Wentworth's eyes narrowed and his heart's beats quickened. There was youth in the tension of that woman's body, despite the shawl and the old woman's dress. The gleam of those eyes....

"Come, come," said Wentworth to the youth sharply. "I asked you for a match."

The youth with the knife snarled an oath and leaped forward. Wentworth's cane whipped across and steel rang, flew against the wall and rang again. The tough reeled back, clutching his wrist. Wentworth sprang after him. The head of his cane smashed upward against the fellow's jaw, slammed him unconscious to the pavement. Then Wentworth had his back to the wall beside the woman.

"I told you not to do this, Nita," he said softly. "It's dangerous enough for one of us...."

"To your left, Dick," the woman said coolly. Her voice was not old. It was a soft and husky contralto and there was a joyous note in it. There was no doubt now. It was Nita, Nita van Sloan, the Spider's sweetheart, who had come to help him in his Underworld crusade!

WENTWORTH'S CANE slid out in a rapier thrust and clicked against the forehead of a man creeping in upon him. The fellow staggered back, shouldered the wall and rolled down it to the pavement. Another sprang forward, with a blackjack. The cane swung in a swift arc, cracked against the man's ear, and at the same instant the woman fired a pistol, twice. The two men who remained on their feet fled in wild disorder, their feet slapping the pavements hard, their bodies crouched far forward.

"Get a taxi, Nita!" Wentworth snapped the words as he jerked his automatic from its holster. He'd give these rowdies something to remember. He heard Nita's feet beat hurriedly away, then he fired twice in quick succession toward the men. Even as he pulled the trigger, sending screaming lead after the men, two spurts of ruddy flame lanced from a dark doorway across the street. His automatic swung toward the spot, but he held his fire. The shots had not been aimed at himself.

The two fleeing men whose heels he had meant to burn with bullets pitched forward to the pavement. They hit heavily and rolled together, into a dark, formless bundle. *They* had been the targets of those mysterious shots. Wentworth knew that one of his bullets, aimed low, had ploughed into a falling body....

As he stared toward the doorway, a stately figure stepped from the dark, a man in a tall silk hat. Wentworth started forward with ready gun, then checked, sucked in his breath.

The man was—the Underworld leader himself!

The man paid no attention to Wentworth, but walked on until he stood over the bodies of the two dead men. He pressed the ferrule of his cane to the cheek of one. A sizzling sound reached Wentworth's ears and as he advanced closely, his nostrils quivered with the stench of burning flesh!

Wentworth cursed, sprang forward, and the other lifted the ferrule of his cane. He wore still the disguise of Judge Scott, but he had drawn a cape about his shoulders so that the gory chest was hidden.

"The other kill is yours," he said smoothly, in his deep grave voice. "I can't abide these street toughs who molest women."

A strange anger sent a wave of heat over Wentworth's body. The gang chief—a super-criminal and sponsor of a dozen deliberate murders—had shot down toughs, and Wentworth found himself enraged at the action. But he made no move to shoot. He tucked his cane under his arm and spilled the diffused rays of a small pocket flashlight on the dead. His light revealed a small brownish burn on the face of the slain man. It was in the shape of a small violin!

WENTWORTH JERKED his shoulders. He realized abruptly that this man could just as easily have killed him also. That he had chosen, instead, to strike down these other men.

A stiff smile lifted Wentworth's lips. He pocketed his flashlight and drew out a small platinum cigarette lighter which he pressed to the forehead of the other dead man.

As he straightened, the gang leader dropped his gaze to the spot Wentworth had touched and slowly, he, too, smiled.

On the paling flesh of the dead crook's forehead glowed *the seal of the Spider.*

"Ah," said the Underworld leader gently, "the Spider."

"Yes," said Wentworth softly. "Can you think of any reason why I shouldn't kill you?"

The other still smiled. "Not a single one."

Wentworth's smile gave way to a frown. He jerked his head impatiently. The man had a valid plea and he did not make it. He had stood passively by when he might have shot Wentworth and Nita, had entered the battle in their behalf at the first moment

34

he could be sure his bullets would not fell the wrong person. He knew that, yet he said nothing.

And Wentworth knew that, quite aside from the fact that he still had no clue to the man's organization, he could not shoot him down in cold blood, as he deserved.

"Those were your men," Wentworth said harshly.

"Yes, they were."

"But you helped me instead of them!"

The gang chief shrugged. "As I said, I do not approve of street toughs who molest women."

"But that gives you a very definite claim upon me not to harm you," Wentworth said sharply. "You deliberately spared my life."

The false face of the chief opened in a laugh. "I tell you frankly that if I had known who you were, I would not have spared you."

Wentworth looked into the man's eyes and a grim smile twisted his lips. He hated all criminals with a bitter and undimmed hatred, yet this man merited respect. He was a fair and courageous enemy.

Clearly he was a gentleman. Once more, a man of strength and power had run amok. But because of these very qualities he was the more dangerous to humanity.

Slowly Wentworth lifted his automatic until it bore on the heart of the other. The chief's gun was in its holster, hidden beneath his buttoned coat. But he still smiled steadily into Wentworth's eyes.

There were reasons for not killing the man, of course. His personality was the only clue to the machine which was throttling the city with its demoralizing grip upon the police and the courts. If this man died, there would be no trail to follow. On the other hand, his death would remove an intelligence of incalculable value to the Underworld, menace to the upper....

"Thanks, Spider," the man laughed, "I'll remember that you spared my life. Some day I may reciprocate."

He started to stroll away, lifting his hat in mark of extreme respect, swinging his cane. Before Wentworth had been fully aware of it himself, the man had read in his eyes the decision not to kill!

"Wait!"

The other halted, turned, his head bowed attentively.

"While we are being strictly honest," Wentworth said sharply, "let me tell you—it's only the fact that I believe your death would hinder more than help me in eliminating your organization, which saves you."

"Nice of you to say that," the other responded in his gentle, suave voice. "I appreciate your attempting to release me from the obligation. But, Spider, the truth is this: you are too much of a gentleman to shoot another gentleman in cold blood."

Wentworth took a brisk step forward. "You may be right, but I'm going to have a look at your face!"

He lifted his hand to rip off the disguise, and heard a sharp footfall behind him. He sprung aside, jerking up his gun—

Too late. One of the men he had knocked out was already upon him with a club. Wentworth squeezed the trigger, but the club caught his forearm in the same instant. His gun clanked to the pavement, the bullet went wild. A second blow caught him on the forehead. His memory went dead as the dark pavement rose to meet him.

CHAPTER 4
THE SPIDER'S VISIT

WENTWORTH RECOVERED consciousness with his head in Nita's lap, cold wind whipping his face from the forward rush of the taxi. When he had recovered fully, they left that taxi, walked westward several blocks before they caught another. They did that twice more, before Nita left Wentworth to enter an old rooming house.

As he waited at the mouth of an alley, he frowned at the pounding ache in his head. If he closed his right hand, red-hot pincers tore at the muscles of his forearm. There was an ugly bluish lump on his forehead. It was pain even to think, but he must....

Nita had trouble locating a taxi, she had told Wentworth, and had returned just as the man clubbed him to the pavement. She had charged forward, shooting, but the tough and the gang chief had ducked into a dark doorway. She had then persuaded the taxi driver to help her with Wentworth.

"Persuaded?" Wentworth had asked curiously. Her answer had been to expose an automatic in her palm.

Wentworth reviewed these things as he waited for her now.

Within ten minutes, she emerged from the black mouth of the alley. She was as vastly changed as Wentworth had been when he had discarded the disguise of Limpy Magee.

37

Her furred suit was modeled exquisitely to her slender figure and a jaunty Pied Piper's hat sat upon her curly hair. Now at last she was herself, Nita van Sloan, whose face and name were well known in the highest circles of the city's society and who, alone among women, knew the Spider's secret.

Wentworth ordered the new cab driver to hurry to Police Headquarters. He stripped off all disguise and leaned back, eyes closed, on the cushions. Nita sat erectly beside him, holding his hand in both of hers while he told her with concise phrases what had happened in Collins' saloon.

As always, when he was with Nita there was a strange mixture of joy and sorrow in his heart. Joy in her presence, sorrow that they could never be more to each other than this. For the Spider could not marry, not while death and disgrace might drop a halter about his neck at any hour of day or night. Not while Underworld and police hunted him with drawn guns.

Both Underworld and forces of the law hated him with an equal fervor. The criminal hate was born of his untiring efforts to purge their ranks. The police hated him for his uncanny speed of action, for his solution of gigantic crimes that put to shame their most furious efforts. He made a mockery of their best men by his ability to seize their prey before they even suspected who that prey might be. Technically, the Spider was a murderer who boasted of his kills by printing a glowing red spider-shaped seal upon the foreheads of his prey. It did not matter that he killed only those who deserved to die.

These things were a barrier to the love of Nita and Wentworth and he had struggled desperately to put her from his mind and heart. But love had proved stronger than his will. He had told Nita of his work, and, far from turning her from him, the altruism of his thankless and untiring labor for humanity had drawn her into his arms. They had pledged, together, an undying fight against the criminal foes of mankind.

BUT WENTWORTH had forbidden Nita to follow him into the Underworld on his latest crusade. The Underworld had turned too brutal, too fearless. Robbery, murder, rape were rife. The series of brutal murders that had been committed during the last thirteen weeks, regularly every Thursday night at eleven-thirty o'clock, was another phase of the criminal revolt. Then there were the amazingly spectacular and successful robberies, with a loot totaling well over a million. The hellish part of it all was the utter collapse of legal machinery—the all-powerful political protection afforded for the offenders.

No, Wentworth did not want Nita to enter the Underworld. But she had persisted, assuming the disguise of an old peddler woman, to seek information that would help the Spider in his fight. As Wentworth finished his recital, Nita squeezed his hand.

"I, too, have learned something," she said quietly. "This new leader of the Underworld calls himself the Death Fiddler."

Wentworth frowned, then smiled tightly. That, then, explained the violin brand that he used....

Without warning, Nita was thrown against him. The taxi whirled unexpectedly to the left, tires shrilling. The driver twisted a white face about.

"Gang had the street blocked," he called back in explanation. "Saw 'em just in time."

Wentworth nodded, his lips grim. This was the sort of thing that went on all the time. Police apparently helpless. Insurance companies raising their premiums for robbery insurance.

"It's damnable that police can't stop this sort of thing," Wentworth said to Nita thinly. He shook his head, shrugged. "You didn't learn the significance of that man being called the Death Fiddler?"

Nita shook her head. "I think it has something to do with a symbol that is used among members of his band."

Wentworth smiled mirthlessly. "The Death Fiddler and his band," he murmured. "They're making the city dance to their music, right enough. Murder music!"

The taxi squealed to a halt before the Center Street Headquarters and Wentworth escorted Nita up the steps. In the light of the doorway, the two had an aura of vitality and well-being. It was something more than the perfection of their clothing, the jauntiness of their carriage.

Nita's gaze was quiet and unafraid despite the perils they had been through. She was a poised woman of the world; her head of clustered chestnut curls was carried high and proudly; there was

LIMPY MAGEE

RICHARD WENTWORTH

dignity as well as beauty in her face. Her brow bespoke wisdom, and clear courage was in the modeled firmness of her red lips.

Wentworth was lithely built, powerful without bulk. Ready strength was in the swing of his broad, perfectly tailored shoulders; a touch of arrogance lay in the poise of the well-shaped head. His face was vital, and indisputable charm lurked in the direct gray-blue eyes as well as the mouth, with its hint of quiet humor. There was a set to the lean jaw that meant his lips could be thin and bitter, too.

A carrot-topped policeman jumped to open the door of the Commissioner's private office and Wentworth acknowledged the service with a brief, "Hello Cassidy."

The Commissioner, Stanley Kirkpatrick, rose to greet them with a grave smile. The room was large and square, high ceilinged, sparsely furnished, the carpet soft underfoot.

Kirkpatrick retired behind his desk again when he had seated the two. He leaned back, and his keen blue eyes had a frosty sparkle. If he noticed the welt on Wentworth's forehead, he gave no sign.

"When did you two get back from Canada?" he asked. His lips, beneath the spike-pointed, military mustache, were sardonic.

WENTWORTH RETURNED the smile blankly. That was the story he had given out when he had quit his Fifth Avenue apartment for the Underworld, and Kirkpatrick knew the story was a falsehood. Kirkpatrick knew beyond any question that Wentworth was the Spider, had told him so to his face. But there never had been any final proof of his knowledge. Furthermore, Kirkpatrick admired and respected this killer of the night who struck swiftly where the law's machinery, for all Kirkpatrick's brilliance, could move only with a cautious tread. And he had declared an armed truce with Wentworth.

When he could, he would help the Spider in his battles against the Underworld. But if ever there came a time when proof was put into his hands, he would act with full power and brilliance of which he was capable, even if it meant sending his closest friend to the electric chair. That was why there was a sardonic smile on his lips as he asked now about Canada, knowing full well that Wentworth had been about the work of the Spider.

"The hunting was boring," Wentworth said with a smile, "and I never did care for fish."

Kirkpatrick laughed. "What brings you here?"

Wentworth nodded pleasantly. "I heard that a fellow called the Death Fiddler was cutting up high jinks here, murdering police and one thing and another, so I thought I'd give you a hand."

Kirkpatrick's blue eyes narrowed. "So he calls himself the Death Fiddler, does he? Thanks, Dick."

The two men faced each other with the wary smiles of fencers, Wentworth's lean, tanned face blankly innocent. Kirkpatrick's shrewd, with eyes narrowed, lips pursed beneath his military mustache. He had a saturnine face, cut deep with creases of determination and humor. Black hair lay straight and flat upon his crown, stippled with silver at the temples. A gardenia graced the lapel, typifying his immaculate dress.

Nita laughed, a little uncertainly. "There's something going on here that doesn't quite meet the eye," she said. "What are you two fencing about?"

Wentworth raised his brows. They were tilted upward quirkily and when he arched them they were mocking. "Nothing at all, dear," he said blandly.

Kirkpatrick closed his lips more firmly. The smile left his

face. "Things are much more serious than I dare admit," he said, his words clipped and precise. "Fifty police have been killed by bandits in the past two weeks. Three have been shot down tonight and another man is missing…."

"That last wouldn't be one William Horace, would it, Kirk?"

Kirkpatrick stiffened perceptibly. His fingers, forming a neat tent above the blotter, whitened with pressure.

"This is no time for joking, Dick," he said sharply. "If you know anything about Horace, tell me."

Wentworth nodded amiably, drew a platinum and black cigarette case from his pocket. Kirkpatrick glowered at him for a moment, then shrugged and accepted a cigarette when the case reached him. Wentworth deliberately lighted all three cigarettes from the single flame of his lighter. He snapped it out, set down and nodded.

"I'm not joking," he said calmly. "I want a special favor, Kirk. I want you to give me a letter assigning Horace to secret duty of some sort, ordering him not to reveal the fact that he's alive even to his own mother, if he has one…."

"He has one," Kirkpatrick interrupted. "She lost her husband in a gun battle with bandits seven years ago on the same beat her son has now."

"Bill seemed like a nice boy," Wentworth said mildly. "His mother must be told you have hope, but that Bill disappeared from his post. You are doing everything possible to locate him…."

Kirkpatrick was abruptly on his feet. "Listen, Dick," he said harshly. "This is no time for trifling. If you know where Bill Horace is, out with it!"

Wentworth continued his suave smile. "I haven't said that I know," he pointed out. "I think that presently, you will receive a telephone call, possibly anonymous, which will inform you that one Limpy Magee, operator of a second-hand shop on Clancy Street, shot Horace through the head in Collins' back room, and afterwards carried the body away in his car. But not having established *corpus delicti* you will have difficulty in doing anything to Limpy Magee."

Kirkpatrick frowned and slowly dropped back into his seat.

"I tell you," Wentworth continued, "that it's important for the Underworld to believe Bill Horace dead, and for you to assign him to secret duty so that he will continue to seem dead." KIRKPATRICK'S EYES were half closed. He lifted a hand to his mustache, fingered it. "I wonder what would happen if we searched this second-hand shop of Limpy Magee," he said softly.

Nita's hands were twisting in her lap, but the smile upon her lips did not vary. She shook her head slowly as if the entire thing was beyond her, not worth worrying about.

"Limpy Magee and a lot of second-hand junk," Wentworth shrugged, "and the wreckage of a plan that might otherwise place this Death Fiddler in your power."

The door opened and Cassidy stuck in his carrot-haired head. "Senator Bigger and some other big shots, Commissioner," he said.

Kirkpatrick frowned, looking at Wentworth speculatively. "Show them in, Cassidy."

Wentworth moved leisurely over behind Nita's chair, and Cassidy threw the door wide. Senator Bigger waddled in behind an immense belly, his fat-swollen face wreathed in smiles, his triple chin jovially creased.

"Hello, hello, Commissioner!" he boomed heartily. "I hope we aren't intruding on anything important!"

"Just a social call," Kirkpatrick assured him, standing straight behind his desk, face grave. "You know Mr. Wentworth and Miss van Sloan." The politicians bowed and Kirkpatrick asked shortly, "What can I do for you?"

His dislike of the politician and his kind was very apparent. Politicians were responsible for the freeing of many prisoners, the destruction of the police morale. And that was why so many of his men—his boys, he called them—were being killed.

The senator swung his belly about, looked over his shoulders at three other men who had followed him in. The effect reddened his face, beaded his upper lip with perspiration, He wore a black cutaway and dark gray trousers like a reversed tent.

The men behind him were quiet, but smiling. Wentworth recognized them all. Raymond Allen, high in the councils of the local political party; Fuzzy Larson, a congressman; Patrick O'Larry, another senator. They were all big men in their party, Allen perhaps the strongest.

"You speak for us, Senator," Allen urged Bigger, his voice soft.

Bigger cleared his throat, glanced at Nita and Wentworth.

"What we have to say may be private, Commissioner! You may not want it to be publicized!"

Kirkpatrick waved his long-fingered hand. "Go ahead."

Bigger cleared his throat, thrust out his stomach. "Commissioner Kirkpatrick!" he began oratorically, "We are here to confer upon you a gr-r-reat honor! The greatest that it is in the power of our proud party to bestow! We come to you because your long service to the pee-pul warrants reward...."

"Come to the point," Kirkpatrick cut in.

Senator Bigger, caught in the middle of a period, stopped talking and puffed. He looked as hurt as a child spanked in public. Kirkpatrick was uncompromisingly stern, his eyes boring into the slightly bulging ones of the senator.

"We want you to accept our nomination for Governor," Bigger finished weakly.

CHAPTER 5
THE DEATH FIDDLER STRIKES

KIRKPATRICK FROWNED. Wentworth saw that refusal of the offer was imminent, and stepped forward.

"I can see that the Commissioner is overwhelmed," he said smoothly. "There is no doubt that he well deserves the honor you offer, but he has never sought public reward for his services." Wentworth paused and shot a sidewise glance at Kirkpatrick. The Commissioner was frowning at him, saturnine face slightly belligerent, eyes puzzled. "You don't mind, do you, Commissioner?" Wentworth asked him humbly.

Kirkpatrick shrugged. "Go ahead," he said grumpily.

And Wentworth did go ahead, with an easy hypocrisy that put the politicians at once at their ease. This was the kind of talk they could understand. Kirkpatrick's bluntness disconcerted them.

"And so," Wentworth concluded, talking more to Raymond Allen than to Senator Bigger, for he knew well who was behind this move, "you understand that the Commissioner cannot at once give you his answer. His services here have meant a great deal to him. He loves his men, but the opportunity for larger services appeals to him. You must give him time to think this over."

Allen's eyes met his and a slight, humorless smile creased his sunken cheeks. He shook hands on departing.

"Very nicely done, Wentworth," he murmured. "If you ever want to go into politics…" He let his voice die out as he turned away, and Wentworth closed the door, then rested his shoulders against it.

"Don't you see, Kirk," he cried, "it's the chance of a lifetime! As Police Commissioner you can suppress petty crime, but you are powerless against the crooks allied with the political powers of the city, such as this Death Fiddler. Your men have brought in a dozen gunmen for the murders of your policemen, and everyone has been turned loose. It's politics that does it!"

"Politics is filthy," Kirkpatrick said violently. "I won't have a damned thing to do with it."

Wentworth nodded. "That's just why politics is dirty," he said. "Because good men won't enter the field. This is the chance of a lifetime, Kirk. From Albany, you can clean up the whole damned state with your police force and your power to appoint investigators."

Kirkpatrick sat down slowly, and Wentworth crossed to him, beat softly on the desk with his fist. "The chance of a lifetime, Kirk!" he insisted.

Neither was conscious of the door opening, but, looking up abruptly, Wentworth saw a man standing unobtrusively against the partition, his sleekly blond head respectfully bowed, his eyes on super-polished shoe tips.

"I'm sorry," he said gently, "but Cassidy was out of the office and I knocked and took the liberty of stepping in since I had an important communication."

He lifted his eyes for a moment, a slight smile on his lips, and Wentworth was struck with the intense blue of the man's gaze. Kirkpatrick gestured impatiently.

"All right, Larrimore. Let's have the message."

The man toed soundlessly to the desk, placed on it an official looking envelope. Kirkpatrick ripped it open.

"There may be an answer, I was told," Larrimore said.

ABRUPTLY WENTWORTH identified the man. He was Dodson Larrimore, secretary to the Mayor. He wore carefully creased clothing, but he was as inconspicuous as a female robin. Even while he stood there, eyes carefully on polished shoe tips, one almost forgot that he was in the office.

Kirkpatrick tossed the letter vehemently to his desk. A dull red suffused his cheeks. When he spoke, his voice was quiet, but the tight gripping of his fingers on the chair arms showed how great was the effort at self-control.

"Who is the Mayor planning to appoint in my place?" he asked.

Larrimore said, "I beg your pardon?"

Kirkpatrick snorted, repeated his question, then held the letter out to Wentworth.

It requested Kirkpatrick's resignation as Commissioner, effective at once. There was no explanation. Kirkpatrick, as the Mayor's appointee, was subject to removal at any time.

Larrimore said slowly, looking directly at Kirkpatrick: "Do I understand that the Mayor is asking you to resign?"

"You do!"

Larrimore flushed. "It isn't right, sir," he said, the subdued quiet dropping from voice. "Why, you're the best Commissioner the city has ever had...."

Kirkpatrick smiled quizzically at Larrimore. "I've been expecting it for some time," he nodded. "Purviss never liked me and I've refused a half dozen 'favors' for his friends recently."

NITA VAN SLOAN

Larrimore was obviously excited. He forgot to keep his eyes on his shoe tips. "That isn't what Commissioners are for!" he declared. "Can't you do something, sir? Is there anything I could do for you? You got me my job, sir. I won't ever forget that, and…."

Wentworth smiled. Such gratitude was pleasant. Larrimore was about thirty, a clean-cut man with solid strength in his face.

There seemed no doubt of his sincerity. The man was stirred out of his customary secretarial calm.

"I appreciate it, Larrimore," Kirkpatrick interrupted, "but forget it. I'm afraid my usefulness as Police Commissioner is about ended anyway. When there is hostility between this office and the Mayor, nothing good can come of it." He shrugged slightly, parting his mustache with thumb and forefinger. Then he nodded, picked up the phone.

"Get me Senator Bigger's apartment, please," he directed, "and have him call me as soon as he returns home." He leaned back in his chair and rocked on noiseless springs; his eyes on Larrimore's flushed face.

"I'll dictate my reply in just a moment, Larrimore," he said quietly.

Wentworth leaned forward and clapped Kirkpatrick on the shoulder. There was quick jubilation in his veins. In his last crusade, Kirkpatrick had narrowly escaped being accused of helping the Spider, and Wentworth had feared for his future reputation. If he became Governor, Wentworth would have a newly energized police force to fight in the city, but he would be relieved of constant worry about his friend.

THE PHONE buzzed softly, and Kirkpatrick snatched the instrument.

"Senator?" his voice rang. "I'm accepting your nomination for the governorship, and I'll issue a statement to the papers at once in the form of a letter to the Mayor... I appreciate your offer, Senator, but I'll map my own campaign. Thank you."

Answering a buzzer, a young man in civilian clothes entered and seated himself with pencil poised over a notebook.

"Type this letter at once and make six carbons," Kirkpatrick said briefly. "You will then give a copy to the representative of each newspaper and bring the original to me for immediate signature. This letter goes to the Mayor.

> Dear sir:
>
> I submit herewith my resignation as Commissioner of Police, effective tomorrow, as per your request.
>
> I am convinced that you are motivated by dirty politics. It may interest you to know that I am running for Governor in the Fall election, with the express purpose of cleaning up your administration.
>
> I would like to point out that in the recent outbreak of crime and murder, the police have made many arrests only to meet with defeat in the courts. A number of these releases of prisoners were made by your appointees to the magisterial bench.
>
> I ask you, furthermore, if you can affirm truthfully that you had no previous knowledge that these prisoners would be released?
>
> Yours for clean government,
>
> Stanley Kirkpatrick.

Larrimore's smile grew during the dictation, but at the last savage sentence, he started and frowned.

The secretary who was taking the letter looked big-eyed with amazement. He fairly ran from the room.

"Do you really believe he had a hand in all this crime, sir?" Larrimore asked slowly.

Kirkpatrick grunted. "Can't say. But what I pointed out in the letter is a fact. It at least merits explanation."

In an incredibly short time the typed letter was on Kirkpatrick's desk. Kirkpatrick read it over with bent brows, lips pursed. Then he signed it with a heavy flourish, dropped it into an envelope.

"There's your answer, Larrimore."

Larrimore bowed, said, "Thank you, sir," thrust the envelope into his pocket, and tip-toed from the room, followed by Kirkpatrick's stenographer. Kirkpatrick's face, turned toward Wentworth, was suddenly tired and drawn. His shoulders slumped a little.

"This is the reward for doing a job well," he said heavily.

Wentworth clapped him on the shoulder. "The wisest move you ever made in your life," he declared. "As for reward, surely you didn't expect any?"

Kirkpatrick acknowledged that with a slight shrug, looked up at Wentworth quizzically. "You should know, eh, Dick?"

Yes, the Spider should know. He gave up his life, his every chance of happiness to the service of humanity—and his reward was that humanity hounded him with threats of death. But he only smiled at Kirkpatrick's query.

"The knowledge is scarcely esoteric," he said. "Don't you want to give me that letter to Bill Horace now as one of your last official acts?"

KIRKPATRICK LAUGHED sharply. "You never give up, eh, Dick?"

He drew a sheet of paper toward him, scrawled an order, handed it over. "By the way, I heard from Corcoran the other day. He and Annie sent their love. They've got a little girl."

Wentworth slid the letter into his pocket a with a mechanical smile. Corcoran was Kirkpatrick's only nephew. He had married a girl who had been the pawn in one of Wentworth's battles with the underworld, and they had a child....

Nita's hand touched his arm "Come along, dear. Kirk will have a lot to do tonight."

Wentworth nodded, moved toward the door.

"Oh Dick," Kirkpatrick called, "I forgot to tell you that the Spider called me tonight...."

Wentworth turned at the door, eyebrows raised.

"He warned me," Kirkpatrick went on, "that Judge Scott was to be murdered tonight, and advised a guard. Another thing. Just before you called, a kill by the Spider was reported, just around the corner from Limpy Magee's shop."

"That's a coincidence," Wentworth said lightly.

"I'm not so sure of that," Kirkpatrick told him, leaning forward on his desk, "but this is the curious thing. Beside this man the Spider killed and branded was another corpse, branded with a violin. I was wondering whether that violin brand could have anything to do with—the Death Fiddler!"

Wentworth frowned, nodded. "Yes, it does. I intended telling you that a violin was his brand. Why he doesn't mark the men he kills on Thursday nights, I don't know."

"I'm glad the Spider's busy again," Kirkpatrick said softly. The eyes of the two men met. Into the understanding silence that fell between them rolled the single chime of a distant bell. Kirkpatrick started, glanced at his watch.

"Eleven-thirty," he said tightly. "I hope those guards at Judge Scott's place are alert."

Nita's hand touched Wentworth's arm and he covered it with his. The three of them were tense, waiting for the word that soon would come of the Death Fiddler's failure or success. When the telephone buzzed, their tight muscles jerked. Kirkpatrick's hand went out slowly to the instrument.

"Kirkpatrick speaking," he said. "Yes." Slowly his lips compressed, the lines at his mouth corners deepened. "Yes, I'll go there." He hung up, lifted his eyes to Wentworth's.

"They got Judge Scott, all right. Machine gunned him through a window while he was playing bridge, and got clean away. They also burned down a butler and three detectives I had on guard."

CHAPTER 6
$20,000 KIDNAPING

THE NEWS struck Wentworth with the force of a physical blow. He had counted heavily on the police guard protecting Judge Scott—had hoped through that means to build up their morale, already badly shaken. But the Death Fiddler had proved too clever for them.

A jagged curse rasped in his throat. His fists knotted at his sides.

Nita's hand left his arm. "I'll wait here," she said. "You go."

Kirkpatrick shook his head. "That's not where I'm going," he said. "I'm going out on something you don't know about yet, Dick. The Fiddler demanded a hundred thousand dollars from John K. Barnfeller...."

"The devil he did!"

Kirkpatrick nodded. "And when Barnfeller refused to pay, he said he would kidnap him tonight and hold him for *two* hundred thousand."

"Calling his shots, eh?" Wentworth's face showed excitement. "That takes nerve and excellent organization. You're going to Barnfeller's home?"

"No." Kirkpatrick was worried. "Barnfeller's secretary just phoned the sergeant downstairs that, defying all orders, Barnfeller had left for a downtown conference of bankers. Barnfeller won't take the threat seriously. He has an escort of six armored motorcycles mounting machine guns, two radio cruisers carrying four men each, and two detectives riding in the car with him."

Wentworth lifted his brows. "Barnfeller isn't that important."

"But the morale of the police department is. If the Death Fiddler succeeds in this...."

THE SIREN in the Commissioner's big, low sedan purred now and again as he and Wentworth sped northward through streets almost devoid of traffic. The air was pleasantly warm, with a faint damp promise of rain. A police patrol, four men marching together with guns in their hands, went warily down Fifth Avenue.

"By tomorrow," said Kirkpatrick, "I expect to arm each patrol with a riot gun and a machine gun. They're equipped that way in the worst parts of town now."

Wentworth had to force himself to relax against the cushions. Every nerve was tense, his brain keenly alert.

"If I were going to snatch Barnfeller," he said slowly, "I'd block the road, plant barricaded machine guns to each side, and mow down that guard before they knew what was happening. It would be a simple matter then to take Barnfeller. The Fiddler has no regard at all for human lives."

Kirkpatrick sat erectly as always, the military squareness of his shoulders more emphatic in his tension. He lifted a hand slowly, parted his spiked mustache with thumb and forefinger.

"There isn't any defense against that type of attack," he said slowly, "unless they don't know Barnfeller is out."

Wentworth, lolling back, eyes closed, said: "They probably *caused* him to be called to the conference."

Kirkpatrick's head jerked about toward his companion. "How could they?"

Wentworth's shoulders lifted in a slight shrug. "They're powerful enough to secure the release of criminals in the courts, possibly to obtain your removal—though I'm guessing about that of course. So why not the other?"

Traffic dwindled further as the powerful sedan whipped through Harlem, hissed with mounting speed northward toward the city limits. The thin wailing of motorcycle sirens slowed

them finally and they caught the
distant grouped lights of the Barnfeller motorcade.

Kirkpatrick ordered his driver to
turn about and await the approaching motorcade. They were halfway
in the turn when the crashing roll of
machine guns broke out. Wentworth
saw a steel-sided truck lurch out of
a side street and halt squarely in the
path of the police guard.

Without awaiting orders, the police chauffeur whirled Kirkpatrick's car toward the barrier. The flickering orange fire of a
machine gun danced from the truck and the sedan's front tires
exploded. The bulletproof windshield frosted with radiating
cracks. Fighting the pull of the flat tires, the chauffeur pushed
slowly on toward the truck. Bullets beat a devil's tattoo over the
sedan. Two jarring explosions sounded ahead.

Kirkpatrick snatched at the door handle, but Wentworth
pulled him back with a tight smile.

"No use committing suicide, Kirk," he shouted above the
roll of guns.

The sedan halted with a jar and a scrape of iron.

"We're against the truck," said Wentworth.

HE CRAWLED into the front seat of the sedan, where the
driver sat white-faced and motionless. A crank eased the windshield down an inch at the top, and Wentworth peered upward
at the side of the truck. Machine guns were trained along each

side of the sedan and men kept hungry watch. From beyond the truck still came the chatter of guns.

Wentworth drew both automatics and rested them on the top of the windshield. They blasted together and the machine gunners pitched backward out of sight. Instantly, Wentworth flung from the sedan, vaulting to the running board of the truck. He wrenched open the door, fired twice more, hurled inside as the driver collapsed across the wheel.

A yank, and the man tumbled to the floor. Wentworth peered through a gun port, and his face went white.

Barnfeller's sedan lay on its side, its understructure torn by an explosion. The street was strewn with blue-uniformed bodies. The six motorcycles were sprawled in abandoned postures, smashed against building walls and telegraph poles, the crews collapsed in their seats.

One detective cruiser had rammed the truck, and its windows, which were not bulletproof, lay in jagged ruin upon the bodies of the four men who manned it. The other cruiser had been blasted by a bomb and lay upon its side. In all that street, no man moved.

Wentworth straightened slowly from the loophole, and clambered back to the street. Kirkpatrick stood by the hood of the truck. Silently, the two men met each other's eyes. Kirkpatrick struck the fender heavily with his fist.

"By God, those murderers shall die!"

Wentworth smiled tightly. "You're not Commissioner any more, Kirk—thanks to the Death Fiddler."

The mirth on his lips found no echo in his heart. This was the most overwhelming criminal attack the Fiddler's regime had made. Twenty policemen had been murdered at one blow, and one of the world's wealthiest capitalists kidnaped on the streets of New York. Coming on the heels of the other brazen crimes, it portended fearful happenings.

New York would soon be like a city in wartime, armed guards patrolling all its vital points. Respect for law was no more. There was not even fear. Already newspapers carried reports of plans for further increases in the already augmented insurance rates. Business would be ruined if this continued. And there was nothing at all to prevent the Death Fiddler from pillaging and looting until he had stripped the city bare.

Obviously this new Underworld chief was more clever, more daring than any other criminal Wentworth had ever fought. Even the Fly, who so narrowly had missed defeating the Spider, had not dared to direct his raids in person as this man did, nor flaunt his scheduled murders by mockingly appearing in the habiliments of the men he intended to kill! The Fiddler did not even trouble to hide!

He must—Wentworth's fists knotted at his sides—he *must* kill this Fiddler. An end to truce! What did it matter if he didn't know the man's organization? He would find and smash that, just as he would kill the Fiddler himself. Never again would he neglect such an opportunity as he had had in Collins' saloon— not even if it meant his own death!

It was hours later that Wentworth escorted Nita to her home, and returned heavily to the alley which led to the back door of Limpy Magee's. Once within the shelter of its basement, he rapidly resumed the greasy garments of his disguise. He bushed his eyebrows, created a bulbous nose with putty. His hair became frowsled and he fastened to his knee a gadget of steel and leather straps, padded with sponge rubber, which would hold his left leg stiff.

Then he limped heavily upstairs to the room where he had left Bill Horace a helpless prisoner. He clicked on the single fly-specked bulb dangling from the ceiling—and stiffened in surprise. The bed lay in a heap on the floor. The headboard to which Bill Horace had been handcuffed was gone, and so was Bill Horace!

Wentworth cursed under his breath. All his well-built plans depended upon Horace remaining out of sight, apparently dead and destroyed by Limpy Magee. And now....

"Hands up!" a man ordered sharply, from behind.

CHAPTER 7
SUMMONED BY
THE DEATH FIDDLER

A S LIMPY MAGEE, Wentworth had nothing to fear from the Underworld. He lifted his hands and pivoted awkwardly on his stiff leg.

In the doorway of the closet, crouched over a gun that quivered in his hand, stood Jerry Horace. Behind him, Wentworth made out the head of the girl who had defied Bill Horace in the saloon—Tony Musette.

"You killed my brother," Jerry said, his voice going thin, "and I'm going to kill you!"

The girl slid out from behind Jerry. "Where did you put the... put him?" she demanded.

Wentworth's disguised face was screwed up in a semblance of fright; his puckered eyes darted from one to the other of his accusers.

He had had small opportunity to observe them in the saloon, but he saw now that the two were formidable. Jerry, seeming even slighter than his five-feet-six as he crouched there over the gun, was white faced with a mixture of anger and fright. Black, curly hair hung down over a pale forehead, and his eyes glared upward under a wrinkled brow.

Wentworth turned his attention to the girl. Her blue eyes were a match for Bill Horace's, glittering with hot lights now. A soft, lovely mouth was thinned with the pressure of anger, and her rather long nose was thin and white about the nostrils.

"Where's Bill?" she demanded. Her hands closed and unclosed at her sides. It would be impossible to convince these two that Bill Horace was alive, Wentworth realized. Furthermore, that confession would end Limpy's hard won prestige....

"You oughta always wear blue, baby," Wentworth told her. "That dress is swell." It was a tight knitted wool, and hugged her rounded figure closely.

Jerry said hoarsely: "Shut up!"

"Is that nice?" asked Wentworth. "I hands the dame a compliment and you...."

"*Shut up!*" Jerry's gun hand trembled violently. "Where did you put Bill?"

"In the basement," Wentworth told him shortly.

"It's a lie!" The girl came closer, her hands clawlike with bright red nails. "We looked in the basement."

Wentworth shrugged. "I'd put him where he couldn't be found easy, wouldn't I?" He was fighting desperately with words. A man whose hand shook like that was much more dangerous with a gun than an experienced killer.

"If you'll go to the basement with me," Wentworth suggested. "I'll be glad…."

Tony Musette shook her head violently.

"Oh, no, we won't," she said. "I'll take that gun and Jerry will go down and look. And if you don't tell the truth…."

WENTWORTH REALIZED abruptly that he would have even more to fear with the gun in the girl's hand.

"I doubt if the boy friend has sense enough to find it—" he smiled slightly at Jerry's snarl—"but I'll tell him where to look. Go down the steps and straight across the basement on a line with the front of the bottom step—that is, at right angles to the stairs themselves. Count seventeen bricks from the bottom and press the eighteenth and a door will open. Bill's in there."

Jerry scowled at him "That basement is thirty feet across. How can I walk a straight line all the way across it?"

Wentworth smiled. "That is what I told you, my friend. I know which brick to press, but it's tough telling you."

Jerry grunted. "Tony, go with me to the door and take the gun."

There wasn't a half second lost in the shift of the gun from hand to hand. Wentworth had no chance at all to seize it. Jerry went down the stairs with quick-thumping feet.

"Don't think I won't shoot," Tony snapped.

Wentworth smiled at her. "I don't doubt it," he said pleasantly. "But it wouldn't be smart. The police…."

"Pooh!" said Tony. "Who's afraid of the police?"

Wentworth shook his head. "You should not interrupt. It ain't polite. I was going to say the police ain't the only ones you'd have to answer to, there is… the *Fiddler!*"

The girl stiffened. "You are not… not one of *them!*"

Wentworth smiled, and the girl's gun sagged. "It ain't wise to make the Fiddler mad, eh?" He lowered his hands, slipped a crumpled pack of cigarettes from his pocket, lighted one.

"Jerry ain't going to find Bill in the basement," he said conversationally. "You'd better let me have that there gun before he finds himself in trouble with the Fiddler."

The girl lowered her eyes slowly to the gun. Then she shuddered, and dropped it to the floor just as the sound of footsteps came slowly up the stairs.

Wentworth listened, with eyes narrowed behind the smoke of his cigarette. Jerry wouldn't come up the steps like that, not if he had failed to find the right brick—which he would, since there was no door in the wall on that side. He would come bounding up angrily. These footsteps were slow and regular.

"Come here, Tony," Wentworth whispered. "If that's Jerry, he ain't alone."

She stared into the darkness of the hallway with widening eyes, then moved furtively toward Wentworth. He himself was no longer smiling. He had used the power of the Death Fiddler

SNAKEY ANNIE

JERRY HORACE

DANNY DAWSON

MAJ. GEN. PATRICK FLYNN

TONY MUSETTE

BILL HORACE

DODSON LARRIMORE

The DEATH FIDDLER

to break a deadlock, but the very fact that the man's influence was so great was a blow.

His hand slid to the automatic beneath his left arm as the footsteps reached the head of the stair and Jerry moved into the pale oblong light from the door. The youth's bottom lip was caught between his teeth.

"Come in, Jerry," Wentworth invited softly, "and come in fast. Let's see who's behind you."

Snickering laughter came from the darkness. "Okay, Limpy," a man said. "I thought this baby's pard had a gun on youse and come up cautious."

Out of the darkness behind Jerry stepped sleek, flashily dressed Danny Dawson. His hands were empty of weapons. His sharp, long-nosed face was creased with a sly grin.

"Thanks, Danny," Wentworth grunted. Turning, he said: "Now you two get. Scram, Tony. Jerry, take a walk."

The girl's blonde head was hanging. She walked heavily toward the door. Jerry paused in the doorway.

"Cheez, Danny," he said, "I hope you won't say anything about this to the Fiddler."

Danny laughed wheezily. "We'll see," he promised. "Well see."

Jerry went heavily down the steps, and Danny patted Wentworth on the shoulder. "You see what being in the Fiddler's band does for you?" he asked. "I didn't even have to pull a rod to handle that guy. Just told him youse was the Fiddler's pal."

Wentworth nodded sourly. "That's swell. Only I ain't a big enough guy to be *his* pal."

DANNY SMILED slyly. "How do you know youse ain't? The Fiddler told me to bring youse to see him."

Wentworth blinked, fought down the joy that rose within him. This was what he had been playing for. This was why he had come to the Underworld, to locate the Fiddler's headquarters. And now he was to be taken there. He gulped, made his face frightened.

"Hell, I ain't done nothing," he said hoarsely. "What's he want to see me for?"

"Don't blame you for being scared," Danny sniggered. "Guess you ain't done nothing he'd punish you for. Fact is, I think he wants to pat you on the back for bumping the cop."

"You think so?"

Danny nodded solemnly. "I'm almost sure."

Wentworth scurried about, putting on a fresh pressed suit, slicking his hair. When he was ready, the electric light was paling under the assault of dawn. He went with Danny down narrow, creaking stairs. The previous night's hint of rain was unfulfilled and the dawn air was chill and bracing.

Both stared up and down the dirty street before they strode briskly westward. Danny saw nothing, but Wentworth did. He saw that the shadow of a certain doorway was thicker than it should have been, and that the shadow moved. Presently, rounding a corner, he saw a man step out of hiding and recognized the broad-shouldered figure of Bill Horace! The policeman was following him.

Wentworth did not at first know whether to worry or rejoice. As long as Horace followed Wentworth, he could not reveal the fact that he had not been murdered. However, Horace had changed to civilian clothing, and in doing that he might have been seen and identified.

Danny led the way to an elevated platform. After a chill wait, shoulders hunched about their ears, the train clattered up and the doors wheezed open.

It was forty minutes of clanking, rumbling progress on the elevated before Danny touched Wentworth's elbow. They got off together. The sun was above the horizon now and its early red rays were burning the frost off the wooden station platform into rising white steam. The boards thumped hollowly under their feet.

Danny hurried to the street, but Wentworth followed more deliberately, thumping unevenly on his stiff leg. He saw a taxi halt almost a block away and wait without discharging a passenger. He cursed under his breath. Bill Horace, beyond a doubt. But apparently he wasn't barging in yet. He wanted to find out where they were going.

Waiting on the curb while Danny sought a taxi, Wentworth made signals at Bill Horace in the taxi. He motioned him back, flapping his hand in the air with a pushing movement. He was forced to cut that short as Danny drove up. Wentworth climbed awkwardly into the cab. He did not know whether Bill had seen his signal, nor whether he would obey if he had. It was clear that the young policeman was suspicious of him, despite the fact that Wentworth had saved his life.

TWO MINUTES later, Danny halted the car on Lenox Avenue. They went up four stories in an automatic elevator and

Danny rapped on the door instead of ringing the bell—rapped in a slow, broken rhythm. The door opened—and Wentworth flinched back, his mouth sagging wide. He was acting as Limpy Magee would, but he really was startled.

The man who opened the door was dressed in a butler's costume, and down one side of his face trickled a line of blood from a bullet hole in his temple. Yet the man stood erect and asked their names in a grave, expressionless voice.

Danny laughed an excited whinny. "Kind of gets youse, don't it?" he asked Wentworth, "no matter how many times youse sees it. This is one of the Fiddler's men dressed like the butler that was killed last night."

Wentworth sidled past the butler with every appearance of fear. But rage was burning in his soul. The Fiddler not only murdered without mercy; he made mockery of the dead. Well, he would answer for that soon, answer with the Spider's lead burning his vitals.

Just as he thought that, hard hands seized Wentworth's biceps and Danny snaked the gun from the holster under Wentworth's left arm.

"Sorry, pard," he apologized, "but the Fiddler's got to be sure of you before he lets you play a piece in his band." He sniggered at his own joke, handed the gun to the butler. "You don't mind, do you?"

Wentworth grunted. "I always feel silly without a rod." He had another thrust under his waistband in the back, hidden by his coat.

They walked into an elaborately furnished living room—the

walls, even the windows covered with silken drapes woven in pale, blended shades. There were no chairs, here, nothing but tables and shaded lamps. On the tables lay effigies of dead men marked with the bloody wounds which had brought about their deaths. Wentworth's swift eyes, darting over them, picked out Dorsey Hampton, the millionaire who, on the previous Thursday, had been strangled to death in his bed. The tongue of this figure was pinched out between clenched teeth, the eyes were swollen in an empurpled face.

There, too, lay the figure of the Inspector of Police who had been stabbed through the throat at his own dinner party. And the gangster who had been shot down on the streets, as well as four others in the distorted attitudes of violent death.

Wentworth made his shoulders shudder with pretended horror. Even through his rage, he could not repress a certain admiration for the man who had devised this means of terrifying his subjects into utter submission. If the reign of death, the weekly killings, did not intimidate them, they were brought into this charnel house....

THE WOVEN silk drape directly before Wentworth parted with a swirling rustle and revealed a man seated in a heavy chair. Before him was a card table spread with cards; a glass stood at his elbow. The man sat beneath a hooded green lamp which threw a ghastly illumination over chair and table. Across his formal shirt front was a stitching of bullet holes, and blood made a black tracery below them. The man's head was topped by a roach of abundant white hair, and there was judicial severity in the set of his mouth.

Wentworth halted, quivering. It was the Death Fiddler, in the guise of Judge Scott. Should he yank his hidden gun and....

Living eyes opened in the face of the apparent dead man and deep-throated words came from it.

"Howdy, Limpy," it said slowly. "Nice work, Danny. You're right on time."

Danny sniggered with pleasure, ducked his head. Wentworth was cold with anger now but he let his shuddering horror continue. He was supposed to be one of the Underworld's creatures, a little smarter than most perhaps, but far beneath the intelligence of the Fiddler. This show of death was supposed to awe him. He allowed it to, apparently.

"Wh-what do you want with me?" he quavered. The features of the dead judge moved in a stiff smile.

"I am well pleased with you," came the deep, slow voice. "That was nice work you did at Collins' last night."

Wentworth looked pleased. His trembling diminished.

"That was nothing," he said. "I got rid of the body, too. It ain't the first time I killed a man."

The head of Judge Scott nodded. "I may find use for you hereafter," he said. "I brought you here to look at you, to thank you as I could not do at Collins'. Perhaps I shall allow you to become a member of my band." He laughed softly. "When we play, the whole city dances to our tune. Tonight we play for the Bal Masque. There will be rich pickings there for the members of our band."

Wentworth simulated eager greed. The Bal Masque—that

was the ball being given tonight, which was the society event of the season. Jewels worn to the dance would be worth millions....

He nodded eagerly. "I sure would like to join up," he said. "Cripes, when one of your men holds up his left hand... I ain't never seen what they show, but when they do it, everything stands still just like that. Tell me what to do to join up, won't you, chief?"

"All in good time," the Fiddler remarked.

It was an awesome setting—that man known to be dead, nodding and talking beneath the ghastly green light, the bullet holes which had killed him appearing across his shirt front.

"Geez, you had me scared." Wentworth was talking eagerly now, "with all these dead men lying about. That butler was bad, and so was those men over there." He nodded his head at the strangled millionaire, "but when I saw *you*..." Wentworth paused, apparently speechless in admiration.

The sound of a sharp outcry, a tussle and stamping feet behind him whirled him about. He saw the butler go down under a savage gun-blow. Bill Horace, revolver in hand, glared at them from the doorway.

CHAPTER 8
THE FIDDLER CALLS

AT THE challenge of the policeman, Danny Dawson jerked up his hands and stood trembling. Wentworth only stared, apparently paralyzed with surprise. His pulses were throbbing in his temples and there was aching tension in all his body. This was what he had feared, that Bill Horace would crash in and wreck all his carefully laid plans.

He had been invited here to see the Fiddler because the gang leader believed him to have shot down a policeman in cold blood. Now this very policeman was challenging them from the doorway, gun in hand.

Should he snatch out his hidden automatic and kill the Fiddler? But Wentworth didn't know the man's organization yet. Striking too soon would be disastrous. Yet the automatic's pressure under the waist band was comforting. That was a last resort....

Could he break from this place? A curse choked in his throat. How could he get past the policeman's leveled gun? And then what else....

Abruptly, Wentworth laughed. It sounded forced, but that was all right. He wanted it to sound that way. He turned his back on Patrolman Bill Horace and his leveled gun and laughed again.

"Geez, chief," he said to the figure in the chair, "you had me scared proper for a minute there. That's the best of all. He looks exactly like the copper I bumped last night."

Danny's laughter was a whinny. "Cheez," he said shrilly, "you had me fooled, too, chief. I see now. He's just a fake like those bodies on the tables and the butler."

"Keep those hands up," snarled Bill Horace.

The hand of the false Judge Scott came up with a gun and Wentworth flopped down on his face. He heard the policeman's gun blast and, peering upward, saw the chief's body jerk with the beat of lead. Crimson spurted from fresh holes in the stiff-fronted shirt, but the chief's gun kept rising.

A frightened curse from Bill Horace echoed the first shot from the chief's gun, then the door slammed. The policeman had fled. Wentworth got up on his knees, watching red wash down the leader's stiff shirt from the spot where the policeman's bullets had pierced. Wentworth began to curse in a low, monotonous voice. Damn Bill Horace for a fool, he thought. He had killed the Fiddler, frustrated all the Spider's plans….

The Fiddler laughed.

Wentworth jerked up his head and stared at the man, while the laughter continued. Wentworth sprang to his feet.

"Cheez!" he cried. "I thought he'd rubbed you out!"

Wentworth's mind was racing. How in the name of heaven could the man laugh when blood was pouring from five surely mortal wounds in his chest? The laughter stopped and the deep, grave voice spoke as deliberately as before.

"Danny, I thought Limpy Magee killed Patrolman Bill Horace."

"He did, he did!" chattered Danny. "I saw him put a slug right through the bull's forehead. Cheez, *youse* saw him do it."

Wentworth let his eyes go wide with amazement. "You mean… you mean you didn't just put on a show for me. You mean that was really… Oh God, oh God, it *couldn't* be Bill Horace! I shot him through the head and dumped him on a lot in Queens. It couldn't be Bill Horace, it couldn't be."

Wentworth was watching the false Judge Scott closely. Could he convince the man of his terror? The Fiddler's face was expressionless, the eyes shadowed by the position of the ghastly green lamp. The gun was held levelly, pointing at no one.

Once more the Fiddler laughed lightly. "I only sought to test you, my friends," he said softly. "You may go now. You will both hear from me later."

Wentworth stared incredulously up at the shadowed face, then he babbled his thanks and backed toward the door. He was puzzled by the Fiddler's swift about-face, but guessed that the leader did not wish his subordinates to think that a policeman could reach him so easily. Wentworth picked up his automatic from beside the supine butler, but made no attempt to fire at the figure in the chair. If five bullets from a thirty-eight Police Positive had bored that chest and failed even to stop the Fiddler's laughter!…

WENTWORTH LET himself out ahead of Danny and raced limpingly to the automatic elevator, the trembling crook right behind him. They went down staring at each other.

"I don't like it," said Wentworth.

Danny shook his head. "Neither do I. I'm going to get away from here fast. All that shooting…."

They ducked to the back of the building, split up, and Wentworth circled toward Lenox again, seeking Bill Horace. He had to get hold of that rash youngster before he caused any more trouble. Wentworth's lips curved in a tight smile. The cop had courage.

The policeman's taxi was parked near a corner on Lenox and Wentworth slipped up to it, opened the door and climbed in.

"Stow the gun, Bill," he said quietly. "I got a paper for you to read."

Horace said between his teeth: "Hand over the paper and be damned careful about it." The revolver remained against his side. Wentworth passed over the note Kirkpatrick had scrawled. Bill held it to the window and read, then eased the gun away.

"Where'd you get this?" he asked sharply.

"What do you care?" Wentworth asked arrogantly. "You know the handwriting, don't you?"

Bill's silence admitted that. "This says I'm to go after the Death Fiddler and I'm not to let anybody know I'm alive."

Wentworth's lips twisted into a thin grin. "Good! Suppose we go see the Fiddler?" he said softly.

He felt Bill shudder. "I put five bullets in him and he bled and kept on talking," the policeman said in a muffled voice. "What the hell's the use of bucking up against anything like that?"

"That's a fake of some kind, just like the butler was," Wentworth told him "Let's go and see what it was."

They sat there in silence for a few minutes. The early morning traffic was thickening. The frostiness was gone from the air. The taxi-meter ticked on. Wentworth was conscious of Bill Horace's eyes on his profile and he smiled faintly.

"Are you afraid, Bill?" he asked softly.

Bill cursed and his heavy shoulders hunched forward. He slid the revolver into his right hand coat pocket.

"If you can face it, I can," he said thickly.

Wentworth opened the door and stepped out. He paid off

the taxi and, side by side, they strode to the doorway of the apartment.

"I don't see why the cops didn't come," Bill muttered. "All that shooting."

"Probably soundproofed," Wentworth grunted. "Them silk drapes, you know."

The elevator clicked to a stop and Wentworth stepped out into the fourth floor hallway with an automatic in his hand. He crossed directly to the door and rammed it with his shoulder. The door flew in and he dived for the floor, eyes sweeping the room beyond.

It was empty. Silk draperies and tables were gone. So were the effigies of death.

Wentworth sprang to his feet and stared about. Bill was cursing behind him, blue eyes startled.

Wentworth whirled out, hobbled upstairs to the next floor. A woman answered his ring at the apartment just above and looked him over belligerently, brushing hair out of her eyes.

"This is a foine time to be ringing doorbells," she blurted. "And me in the middle of breakfast...."

The room behind her gave no hint of the luxury of the Fiddler's apartment. On the third floor, Wentworth had no better luck. After that he and Bill stared at each other. They went back to the fourth floor apartment and examined it more carefully. In a closet they found seven collapsible tables and a lamp. That was all. The silks and the dummies were gone as completely as was the Death Fiddler and his butler.

"We're licked," Wentworth admitted. "That's the quickest

79

getaway I ever saw. I wasn't out of that apartment more than ten minutes and they got clear."

"I'll find that guy," the cop swore. "Next time I'll choke him. We'll see if he can take that and laugh."

WENTWORTH SMILED faintly, looked at Bill's wrists and saw they had been chafed. "You did a nice job of getting away from those handcuffs."

"Wasn't nothing," Bill grinned suddenly. "I just pulled up my feet and muscled my belly over the head of the bed. Once I got my feet on the floor it was easy to kick out the side pieces of the bed and tote off the head piece. I found a file in your basement and helped myself to some clothes out of your shop. Then I hid out across the street to watch. I figured maybe you had a tie-up with all these holdups, and since you was with Danny Dawson... But you got a note from the Commissioner!"

Wentworth nodded thoughtfully. "You let me know where you're going to hole up, Bill," he said, "and if I get a lead on this guy, I'll let you know."

"Okay," said Horace.

Wentworth walked briskly off down the street. His mind was racing with conjecture. The Fiddler had revealed his plans to raid the Bal Masque tonight very strangely. He was too intelligent to boast needlessly to subordinates. Obviously there had been a purpose behind the statement.

Only one explanation remained. He was not afraid of police interference and he wished to test his new subject, Limpy Magee. If police were informed, he would know that Limpy was not to be trusted. There would be an end of the trail he followed and he would have to start all over again, a new character.

On the other hand, if Wentworth did not inform police of the impending raid, there would be murder at the Bal Masque, a fortune in jewels stolen....

A sudden thought struck Wentworth. Suppose the Fiddler was *not* planning a holdup of the ball, simply intended it as a test? Wentworth shook his head heavily. Whether it was a trick or not, he could not inform police. The very fact that the Fiddler boasted in advance indicated that even a police guard would stand little chance of preventing the raid.

Wentworth's disguised lips thinned. He knew suddenly that he would not inform the police. The Spider would attend the Bal Masque tonight. Let the Fiddler attack if he dared!

CHAPTER 9
THE BAL MASQUE

OUTWARDLY BROADWAY was as gay as ever, decked like a Christmas tree with lights and signs, packed with shuffling crowds and squawking traffic. Outwardly, it was like that. But the spirit of Broadway, the gabbing, happy, noisy spirit wasn't there. The people dragged their feet and their eyes flicked to the shadows where thick patrols of police kept ceaseless watch. When they spoke, their voices were muted. These were people afraid, who sought relief from their fear in thronging with other people.

It was as if the Death Fiddler's murder symphonies spirited upon Broadway from the black fog which shrouded the city. Even the whine of tires on the blackly gleaming asphalt sounded doleful.

Usually the eight police, posted on the two concrete triangles of Times Square where Seventh Avenue and Broadway cross in a gigantic X, would have drawn a throng. Tonight people avoided them. The four traffic police stationed there stood back to back, and each held a machine gun in his arms. At their feet, riot guns rested upon an ammunition case.

All this was intended to bolster the courage of the people, but actually it depressed them. The usual clatter of tongues became a subdued murmur. The raucous barkers in front of motion picture houses seemed to sound unnecessarily loud. A man's normal voice could have been heard easily in the pauses of the automobile traffic. Only the loud-speakers pouring out canned music from the shows were unaffected, and at these police glared resentfully.

In the midst of the gloom-wrapped Broadway section stood the Tory Hotel, house of banquets and balls, facing out on the concrete triangles of Times Square where machine guns pointed vicious muzzles toward the crowds. The austere, age-streaked facade of the hotel rose straight up into the fog, while its roof gardens, under glass at this time of year, pierced the murk with lights which should have been festive.

The street at the side of the Tory was packed, people throng-ing the sidewalk beside its "carriage entrance." Lean-flanked sedans, hearse-like limousines slid up in endless procession, tires purring on the wet pavement. They discharged furred, bedecked,

curiously costumed men and women. The flashlights of newspaper cameramen danced like lightning, flickering intermittent
bluish brilliance over the close-pressing walls and the watching
white faces of the crowd.

It was the night of the Bal Masque.

WENTWORTH'S LANCIA was caught by a traffic
light just east of Broadway. There he sat moodily staring at the
muted throng flocking past. Nita was beside him, her glittering
costume cloaked in ermine and velvet, her glowing hair roped
in diamonds.

She laid a white gloved hand gently on his arm "You're too
somber, Dick," she said softly. "This isn't the way you fight."

Wentworth's lips curved slightly but absently, as his eyes
skimmed the police guard.

"Unless they called out the troops, I don't see how they could
have put a stronger guard here," he said.

That fact should have been reassuring, but Wentworth's spirits
did not lift. He realized that he was battling a criminal leader
who was, at once, the most brilliant and daring one ever to lay
siege to humanity's wealth and happiness. Tonight the battle
was his alone.

Nita's laughter sounded forced. "The Fiddler wouldn't dare
raid the ball. It was just a trick. And you were too smart for him."

Wentworth laughed sharply. Smart! So far all the tricks had
gone to the Fiddler. And he himself did not believe the threatened raid was a bluff.

The traffic lights clicked to green, and the four policemen at
the corner parted the sea of human traffic allowing Wentworth's

car to slide through. His trusted Hindu servant, Ram Singh, at the wheel, brought the long-nosed sedan expertly to the carriage door of the Tory, leaped to the sidewalk, and swung wide the door as he bowed his turbaned head in a profound *salaam*.

Resolutely Wentworth threw off his gloom. Stepping out and turning to Nita, he caught the gleam of the Hindu's eyes and smiled faintly. Ram Singh's oriental soul loved this luxurious display.

As Wentworth held out his hand and bowed Nita from the car, there was a renewed burst of flashlights, a rising murmur from the watching crowd. Both Nita and he were gorgeously attired. The Bal Masque this year had selected the period of Louis XIII: Wentworth wore the garb of captain of the King's Musketeers and Nita was a lady of the court.

Wentworth's attire was strangely symbolic. The curls of his wig, the small, pointed beard and mustache gave him an augmented dignity. His hand rested naturally on the pommel of the dress sword at his waist. His doublet was of royal blue, slashed with scarlet, and his cavalier's hat sported two sweeping white plumes. He looked entirely the part he played in life, a gallant defender of all that was honorable and right.

Nita's gown was pure white, of silken brocade. She seemed to glide forward amid her flounced wide skirts. Above them, her slender body was as graceful as the stem of a flower.

Wentworth concealed worried thoughts behind a smile as they ascended in an elevator with a costumed operator, then bowed and curtsied their way through the great arched doorway to the grand ballroom, where Kirkpatrick hastened toward them, out of the colorful crowd. The Commissioner wore the crimson cap and robe of Cardinal Richelieu. His mustache had been grayed with powder, a dab of whiskers was fastened to his chin.

But Kirkpatrick was anything but gay. "It's queer," he said after the greetings, "but I feel as if there should be a dirge instead of dancing tonight. That damned Fiddler...."

WENTWORTH LOOKED quickly into Kirkpatrick's eyes, then away. He was tortured between a desire to warn his friend what impended, and the certainty that if he did his every chance of tracing the wily and ruthless chief of the Underworld would be destroyed. For the present the Death Fiddler partly trusted Limpy Magee. An alarm tonight before the raid would end that....

He must turn Kirkpatrick's thoughts to other channels. Wordlessly, he proffered a jeweled snuff box and Kirkpatrick partook gingerly.

"No tricks, Dick," he warned.

Wentworth delicately dusted his fingers and sniffed. Kirkpatrick duplicated the feat, and burst immediately into a paroxysm of sneezing.

"You've put—*ka-chew!*—pepper in the damned—*ka-chew!*—stuff!"

"Snuff, my dear ex-Commissioner. Snuff, not stuff," Wentworth corrected mildly. He made his lips smile, but there was no amusement in his eyes. His thoughts were somber. "How's politics?" he asked.

His glance skimmed over the room, scanning flushed and laughing faces. He hoped the evening of revelry would not be spoiled. The lips of the Spider tightened grimly. What panic would seize them if they could read his thoughts! But even Kirkpatrick had failed to do that. He had partly recovered from the snuff now and frowned at Wentworth's question on politics, still pressing a handkerchief to his nose.

"It's a mess," he said, his voice muffled. "Those damned politicians who came last night are dissatisfied with—with—" he fought back a sneeze—"with my resigning. They think I should have retained office until the crime wave, as they call it, has been suppressed. They didn't seem to consider the Mayor's power of removal."

He tried to fight back another sneeze, failed. "Damn that snuff!" he exploded.

"It's powerful," Wentworth agreed. "I suppose the new Commissioner has been appointed?"

"They're going to kick out Boise, if they haven't already," Kirkpatrick said savagely. "That was to be expected, but they're also removing all appointive officials and retiring a lot of the veterans I've trained."

"Who was appointed?" Wentworth repeated.

"Flynn," Kirkpatrick clipped the name off. "It hasn't been announced yet, but he's already busy picking his deputies. Larrimore phoned me. He said he'd be glad to keep us informed of developments. Larrimore will be useful—" He paused, glaring at the floor, went on again with a sarcastic twist of his lips. "Major General Patrick O. Flynn, retired, late of the President's Royal Horse Guards or something. He's reorganizing the police force on a military basis. Military basis hell! He's wrecking it!"

WENTWORTH FROWNED as he toyed with the hilt of his sword. There was a persistent thought at the back of his brain that all this had been planned; that Kirkpatrick's resignation, if not the nomination, had been engineered to achieve disruption of the police force. The Death Fiddler already had the courts well in hand and now he was taking over the police... Wentworth's eyes tightened. If his suspicions were right, it meant that Purviss, or someone with a strong hold upon him, someone like Allen or Senator Bigger....

"Is Flynn here tonight?" Wentworth asked casually. "I see that Allen and Bigger are. I'd know that abdominal protuberance in any disguise."

"Flynn was too busy wrecking the force to attend," Kirkpatrick said sourly, "but you'll find the Mayor about somewhere. Damn Purviss' black soul. I wonder...."

"He hasn't got sense enough to be the Fiddler," Wentworth cut in. "Someone else is pulling the strings. Boss Fogarty could do it."

"He's here tonight," Kirkpatrick said slowly, "Dressed as some duke or another. Ah, there he is."

Wentworth looked at the vigorously erect figure of Boss Fogarty. With a face pinkly florid beneath a wig of long black curls, Fogarty looked far less than his sixty-odd years. Nor did he seem other than the benevolent soul he pretended to be.

Kirkpatrick snorted. "That blackguard takes the city for nearly two million a year one way and another. His word is law throughout the ranks of the party. King of the city, in fact. I can't see why he'd turn to crime."

"How about his son?" Wentworth asked softly.

Kirkpatrick's muscles jerked, his face stiffened into a mask. A man in fool's motley stalked by, gripping his cap-and-bells staff like a club. Kirkpatrick's eyes followed him thoughtfully. A couple circled by in a slow waltz, the girl in a scarlet page's dress, the man in a herald's silver and blue.

A small smile twitched at Wentworth's lips and he lifted a hand to stroke his mustaches. Unless his eyes were playing him tricks—and the Spider's life often depended on the accuracy of his vision—the page in scarlet was Tony Musette and she was dancing with the policeman's brother, Jerry Horace.

"Fogarty's son isn't here tonight," Kirkpatrick said slowly. "Are you serious in suspecting him, Dick?"

Wentworth shrugged. "I suspect everyone, Kirk. Just now I'm wondering what a faro dealer from Gallagan's is doing here with a girl who is a clerk in Macy's."

Kirkpatrick shook his head. "Anyone can come who wishes to spend the money on a costume and pay the admittance. It's a charity affair."

Wentworth scanned once more the thickening galaxy of society and wealth all about him. The room was exquisitely draped in crimson velvet, festooned in garlands of roses. The glow of lights flashed back from a thousand jewels on men's and women's elaborate garments. When and where would the Fiddler strike at all this, Wentworth wondered. Did the presence of Tony and Jerry have any significance?

NITA'S HAND was on his arm. "Dick, you're positively stupid tonight. Come and dance—or shall I accept the invitation of that grand duke who's been ogling me for the last fifteen minutes?"

Wentworth laughed, tried to thrust worry into the back of his mind. "If you accept, the grand duke dies at daybreak with my rapier in his heart," he threatened. "See you later, Kirk."

With a bow, Wentworth escorted Nita to the dance floor and they swung gracefully off on the strains of a waltz. But he stopped as the music ceased on a minor strain, and strolled with Nita toward where Kirkpatrick stood glowering at the floor.

"I wish I'd made Purviss force me out," Kirkpatrick said abruptly.

Wentworth made no reply, but briefly excused himself.

"Where are you going?" Kirkpatrick demanded sharply.

Wentworth raised mocking brows. "Really, Kirk, you do ask the most embarrassing questions."

"Well, isn't that a Police Commissioner's job?" Nita asked. Her silvery laughter rang out with attempted gaiety.

Kirkpatrick's lips relaxed slightly, and as Wentworth left the ballroom, he turned his grave eyes on Nita.

"I'm worried about Dick," he said. "I've never seen him so depressed, so lacking in plans. That business of suspecting Fogarty's son now—he has no reason for that."

Nita smiled and looked away. "Dick has done several things well," she said slowly, "and they have accomplished nothing. You must remember, it's three months and more since these highly organized robberies and weekly murders began. The Fiddler is cleverly protected...."

"Dick has fought things like that before this," Kirkpatrick said swiftly.

Nita nodded. "He has a feeling that there is going to be a raid here tonight."

"A feeling?"

Nita nodded, still looking away from Kirkpatrick. She was aware of his eyes studying her profile, then flicking over the assembled crowd.

"That would be practically impossible," Kirkpatrick muttered.

Nita said nothing more. She watched Tony Musette and Jerry Horace dance by. The girl's lips were smiling, and there was a charming dimple in her chin. She had nice legs and ankles, Nita noticed. No wonder she chose a costume with tights.

Kirkpatrick moved restively. "Care to dance, Nita?"

Nita smiled up at him and they swung out on the floor. Kirkpatrick's costume with its black suit and cape, its cap of crimson, was conspicuous for its somberness among the array of silks and velvets.

"Do you think Dick is justified in his… feeling that something will happen?" he asked.

Nita lifted a smooth shoulder in a slight shrug. "I don't know," she said. "Before I came here tonight, I would have sworn it was foolishness, but Dick's moodiness has begun to worry me. I don't know."

At that instant a man screamed.

THE HOARSE cry ripped through the dulcet strains of the music and stopped it with a discordant crash. Nita and Kirkpatrick froze in the middle of a step, and flung apart, staring toward the middle of the ballroom where a second terrified scream had already begun.

Boss Fogarty stood on wide-planted feet in the middle of a rapidly widening circle of men and women. His right arm was twisted awkwardly up behind him, toward the center of his back. The glistening cream satin of his coat was stained by a lengthening spot of blood. From his back protruded half the blade of a rapier. The other half was buried in his body.

The second hoarse cry choked off and Fogarty went down on his knees, slid forward on his face with one arm still twisted behind him. The rapier's hilt swayed like a flower on its stem. Fogarty's hand clenched hard, then opened limply and dropped to the floor.

It was only then that a woman shrieked. The sound of it rose shrilly, rose until it seemed impossible that a human throat could utter so high and piercing a sound. Then it broke into brittle, shivering fragments.

Not a dozen persons had seen Fogarty fall, but the screams stirred panic everywhere. Women ran headlong for the main doors, some with hands thrust out stiffly before them, others dragging wide skirts.

Kirkpatrick spun toward the musicians.

"Play, men, play!" he shouted.

The instruments made a few wailing sounds, gathered rhythm, then swelled to normal volume. Kirkpatrick hurried to the spot where Fogarty lay. Without touching the flesh he knew the man was dead. Eighteen inches of steel had gone clear through his body.

As the Commissioner straightened, he found a ring of men about him. Women in the background were crying hysterically. One was screaming. The music could not hide the sounds of panic.

From the doorway a deep voice boomed out: "Please, be calm everyone!" it cried. "The police are here."

Kirkpatrick saw a man in civilian clothes striding toward him with two blue-coated police at his heels. The man pushed through the ring, flashed a golden badge in his hand.

"I'm Deputy Commissioner Lyons," he said. "What happened here?" He broke off. "Good God! It's Fogarty!"

Kirkpatrick frowned at him. The man was a stranger to him. Flynn undoubtedly had installed him. The Deputy Commissioner looked sharply about the circle of men and saw Kirkpatrick.

"You are Stanley Kirkpatrick, aren't you, sir?" he asked.

Kirkpatrick nodded. Looking sharply about the ring, Deputy Commissioner Lyons asked if anyone had seen the blow struck. No one had.

"How did it happen," Kirkpatrick asked quietly, "that you got here so quickly, Commissioner?"

Lyons frowned. "Fifteen minutes ago I had a call from a man who said he was an official of the ball. He said a twenty-five thousand dollar diamond necklace had been stolen. I had just arrived to investigate when this murder occurred."

THE MAN was squat of build, thick chested. His voice was heavy and slightly husky. He stood looking at the body of Fogarty, inspecting the hilt of the sword.

"There won't be any prints on that," he said, nodding at the jewel-encrusted pommel."There's just one thing to do."

He drew a deep breath and his face was very serious. "It's going to raise hell, but I'll have to order everyone at the ball searched. The diamonds were stolen from Mrs. Fogarty and it is apparent Mr. Fogarty spotted the thief and was killed to prevent an alarm."

"That's preposterous!"

Kirkpatrick saw that it was Senator Bigger who spoke—as usual in exclamations. The senator thrust out his belly pompously. "Find a man with an empty scabbard! You will have your murderer and your jewels both, then!"

Lyons smiled gravely. "I'm willing to predict there won't be an empty scabbard in the hall," he said. "Furthermore, it would be easily possible for the jewels to have been passed on to an accomplice."

Kirkpatrick, Nita beside him again, was struggling with an impression that there was something wrong about Lyons and his blue-coated officers. Yet on the surface they were authentic enough, his deductions were logical enough.

The Deputy Commissioner turned toward Kirkpatrick.

"Would you mind coming with me, sir?" he asked deferentially. "You're much more familiar with such matters than I and I should appreciate your help."

Nita's hand closed on his arm. "Don't go," she whispered. "That man is a fake."

Kirkpatrick's brows tightened above his eyes. Nita's whisper confirmed his own doubts, though the man's invitation seemed sincere enough.

"Dick expected a raid," she pointed out. "I'm sure that...."

"How about it, Mr. Kirkpatrick?" Lyons asked, his voice sharpening.

Kirkpatrick bowed. "As soon as I've found an escort for madam," he said and gave Nita his arm, guiding her toward a group of women against the far wall. "Do you know anything?" he asked in an undertone.

"One of those policemen," said Nita, "is below the legal requirement for height. He is not quite as tall as I am."

Kirkpatrick continued to bend attentively toward her, but Nita could feel the muscles tighten in his arm beneath her hand.

"You are right!" he said. "I should have noticed that. I knew there was something...."

"This is the attack Dick expected," Nita said firmly. "When they search us, they will take our jewels, make us prisoners and go away."

KIRKPATRICK STRAIGHTENED, flung a glance about the room. Doors and windows were guarded by men in police uniforms. The costumed guests were huddled in flustered little groups.

"I wish Dick were here," he said slowly. "I wonder what's keeping him so long."

"The street is full of police," Nita said softly. "If only we could signal them, this would be broken up in a hurry."

Kirkpatrick laughed. The sound of it was strangely loud in the somber room. "That will be easy," he told her.

They were near a row of chairs against the wall. Kirkpatrick abruptly snatched up one, whirled it around his head at arm's length. His eyes were fixed on a window. If he could smash a chair through it, the commotion should bring at least an inquiry from outside. He had a police whistle between his teeth....

A revolver spoke.

Kirkpatrick swayed, the chair flew from his hands to bounce harmlessly on the floor, then he pitched heavily there himself, flopping over on his back.

Lyons strode toward him on heavy heels, revolver in hand.

"Search this woman first," he ordered sharply. "She probably has the jewels."

Nita dropped upon her knees beside Kirkpatrick, whose eyes were glazing with pain. She scarcely heard Lyons, but two of the false policemen seized her, one on each side, and a sharp pain pricked her arm. She knew that a needle had been plunged into her flesh. Drugs! She opened her mouth to cry a warning. The words did not come. The room spun about her and she slumped forward into the arms of the police.

"All right," Lyons called, "we'll start the search. Ladies first—through this door over here."

CHAPTER 10
SPIDER TO THE RESCUE

WHEN WENTWORTH left the ball, he went directly to a room in the hotel which he had previously engaged and, lighting a cigarette, began to pace the floor. He had already convinced himself that the Fiddler meant to strike tonight, and he sought to figure what method the man would employ.

Certainly the Fiddler would not rush in armed men and line the guests against the wall. There were too many of them. An outcry would certainly be raised before the robbers could get clear. Wentworth shook his head angrily. A dozen other ways suggested themselves, but all seemed equally faulty.

Angrily, he whirled toward a small satchel set upon a rack beside the chiffonier. Snapping it open, he took out a small make-up kit and, standing before the mirror, went to work on his face. Under his deft hands, the skin became taut and sallow, emphasizing his cheek bones. The nose, built up with wax, became beaked and thin, his mouth went lipless. Bushy brows covered his own, and the wig of curls gave place to one of lank black hair. When the work was completed, he carefully inspected himself in the mirror, then nodded briefly.

With quick movements, he doffed his costume. Minutes later, a hunch-backed figure in a long black cape stood in the room, a black, broad-brimmed hat upon his head, sword cane in hand. He switched off the lights and glided to the door.

Now he was the Spider in earnest. The black cape and the hunched back would identify him instantly as that fearsome nemesis of the night.

It had been months since he had ventured forth in the garb. But he felt that the time had come when he must spread once more the terror of his ugly red brand of death.

He peered cautiously through the slitted opening of his door, made sure the hall was empty, then, silent as the killer whose name he bore, made hastily toward the stairs.

He knew the layout of the hotel very thoroughly. A second, smaller ballroom was on the floor above where the Bal Masque was being held. A narrow iron stairway connected with two halls; an auxiliary fire escape and two anterooms of the major dance floor opened on it. Those stairs would provide an entrance for the Spider.

With long strides, he went silently down the stairs to the floor above the grand ballroom. A chambermaid stared at him with wide-eyed amazement, but he walked on without noticing her. She did not scream... had in fact vanished down the hallways when he slid into the smaller ballroom and made his way rapidly toward the anterooms and stairs behind.

ABRUPTLY HE paused, standing stiffly in the middle of the dark and empty room. He had heard a pistol shot in the room below....

With an oath choked in his throat, he flung toward the anteroom stairs. The cane was held lightly in his right hand, its ferrule toward the darkness ahead; his feet were soundless on the polished floor.

At the closed door of the anteroom he paused, listening. No sound came from within. Abruptly the Spider flung the door aside and sprang in, his cane poised like a sword.

A man started up from the head of the stairs, gun in hand, and Wentworth lunged savagely forward.

It was a fencer's lunge, cane before him like a foil, left foot trailing behind, right under him to catch his weight. He covered

97

The Spider's blade struck true toward the Death Fiddler's heart!

fully ten feet in that one bound. His cane tip shot past the leveled gun, crunched home against the man's larynx. A wheezing sound, almost inaudible, was pushed out of the gunman's mouth. He staggered backward with his hands tearing at his throat, tripped, and pitched to the floor. Wentworth flung bodily upon the man's legs so that they would not beat an alarm.

Death came convulsively to the guard and Wentworth eased to his feet, caught up the man's revolver, crept toward the steps. He twisted the head of his cane and drew it away from the stick. There was a singing whisper of steel and the Spider held in his right hand a short, two-edged sword ground to razor sharpness. Gun in one hand, sword in the other, he opened another door and glided down the iron steps.

The platform below was lighted and crouching there tensely were four men, guns in their hands. They were facing two doors which opened off the platform toward the ballroom. At their backs the stairway led both down and up.

Wentworth stole back up the steps, bent over the body of the man he had killed. He pressed the base of his cigarette lighter to the man's forehead, and the crimson of his Spider seal stood out vividly against the purple face.

Wentworth thrust the sword through the edge of his cape, took the captured gun between his teeth and caught up the body. He put a hand beneath each arm pit. Then slowly, on heavy feet, neck corded with the strain of carrying the body in that position, he went down the steps.

He made no effort now to move silently. His solid heels rang dully in the enclosed well of the steps. The stairs curved in a tight spiral halfway down and he rounded this bend abruptly, the body poised before him. It seemed that a dead man walked, a dead man with a face empurpled, with dead eyes bulging like marbles, swollen tongue thrust out—and the dread crimson seal of the Spider on his forehead.

Wentworth heard gasps, a wavering, half-choked cry from the hall below. Then he thrust the body violently from him, so that it dived headfirst down the stairs. Guns blasted wildly; one or two men shrieked in terror. The body struck with a nasty crunch on the iron platform at their feet.

THE INSTANT he thrust the body forward and while the eyes of the men below were still focused on its horrible face, Wentworth leaped backward around the curve. When the body struck, the stairs behind it were empty, but from the darkness above floated flat, mocking laughter. It started softly, a low sinister chuckle, but mounted until the stairwell boomed with diabolic mirth. It ended abruptly, and a hissing whisper dropped from the darkness.

"The Spider is here! *The Spider comes to kill!*"

Once more the bubbling emptiness of his mocking mirth poured down upon them, while men emptied their automatics at the darkness, poured a ringing hail of lead upon the steps—and fled desperately down the stairway.

Wentworth's smile pressed his lips against his bared teeth. He made no effort to pursue the men. It was strange that no one had come from the ballroom to find the cause of that burst of shooting, of those screams and that Mephistophelian laughter. He caught the doorknob and, on the point of entering, dodged back. Curses made his lips writhe. He knew now why no one had come to the help of the guards. He knew now that the Death Fiddler had planned a robbery of the richest ball of years—and how he was going about it.

Anesthetics! The odor he had smelled was chloroform!

The room beyond this door, opening off the ballroom, was filled with anesthetics. Were the victims driven into these rooms and stripped? Wentworth shook his head. He did not know the procedure, but he must disrupt the Fiddler's work. Taking a handkerchief from his pocket and binding it tightly over mouth and nostrils, he yanked open the door, sprang in.

For a second the sight that met his, his eyes staggered him. Women lay upon the floor in neat rows, pale faces turned upward, eyes closed. One swift glance showed him Nita, against the wall, her hair drooping upon her shoulders, the diamonds that had bound it torn away. Even as he entered, another woman, in the doorway, was being stripped of jewels by three men in gas masks, one of whom held a cloth saturated with chloroform to her nose, while another held her arms, and the third rapidly relieved her of necklace and earrings. The men's gas masks covered their entire heads.

Only one of them saw Wentworth at first and he was unable to shout warning to his companions because of the mask. The man dropped the jewels and snatched at his gun.

The automatic in Wentworth's left hand crashed, and the man slammed back against the wall. His shoulders braced against it, he fought frantically to lift his automatic. The other two men whirled at the crash of the shot. Wentworth's gun shot down one, his sword found the other's heart.

The woman they had been robbing, half conscious, staggered aside. The three men slumped to the floor and the door flung wide. A man in a policeman's blue uniform stood in the doorway, gun in hand. Wentworth's lungs were bursting with the need for air as he leaped forward. The policeman's gun blasted.

But the man's eyes were staring wide, his mouth open in surprised fright. He recognized the Spider! The fright made his shot go astray—Wentworth felt it jerk at his cape below his left arm—and before he could shoot again, the Spider was upon him. He went down under the slash of Wentworth's gun and the Spider darted into the ballroom.

Men in police uniforms lined the walls of the room, blocked the windows and the doors. Good God, had he attacked and slain police?

Wentworth's head jerked. Impossible, of course. If police were involved, there would be no chloroforming, no stripping of jewels, no gas masks. Then he caught sight of a man in a deep red cape stretched on the floor—Kirkpatrick. By God, if they had killed Kirkpatrick! A red haze of rage burned his brain.

His angry eyes continued swiftly about the room. Before three other doors, men and women stood in lines guarded by police. They were still and frightened. The musicians were in the line, too—except for the police and the bodies of Kirkpatrick and Fogarty, everyone was in those lines. But no, not quite everyone....

Seated in a chair against the far wall, leaning back at his

ease, was a man from whose chest the hilt of a knife apparently protruded. As he saw Wentworth crouched in the doorway, gun and bloody sword in hand, he lifted his right hand casually and pointed.

"Shoot that man, but don't kill him," he ordered calmly.

There was no doubt that the man was the Death Fiddler.

CHAPTER 11
VICTORY—AND DEFEAT

WENTWORTH GLIMPSED all these things in fractions of a second. Actually he had only darted through the door, halted, and swept his eyes about the room.

At the Fiddler's order, a half dozen policemen threw up their guns. The Spider was too far from the doorway to spring back into its protection. He could not shoot down six men before one of their bullets found his body. There was no possibility of shooting out the lights; hundreds of them shone in clusters on the ceiling. Yet he would not surrender.

A bullet jerked his hat back on his head, and a light, leaden blow burned his right forearm. He spat curses between his teeth. In the brief moment between the instant he dived to the floor and fired his first shots, the Fiddler had disappeared. No one remained except the false police against the wall. Then he was gone, leaping down the fire-exit stairs.

Unexcited voices came to him as he cautiously peered around the wall at the head of the stairs toward the entrance to the grand ballroom. The doors were open, he saw, and once more the prisoners were being ushered out one by one, their jewels stripped from them.

TONY MUSETTE, still brave in her scarlet, stepped through the narrow opening of the doors, her eyes blazing. Jerry Horace was just behind her. A man was on each side of the doorway, two others behind them. The Death Fiddler, a long-bladed rapier in his hand now, stood to one side and watched.

"You hid a ring," one of the crooks snapped at Tony. He snatched the throat of her silken blouse and ripped it. The girl cried out, caught at her torn clothing. Jerry sprang forward with a hoarse shout. His fist connected with the jaw of the assaulter who reeled backward, struck the wall and flopped to the floor.

He wasn't out, but he was groggy. For a moment he lay there, propping himself on an elbow. Then, with a snarled curse, he grabbed for his underarm gun.

The Death Fiddler took a deliberate step forward and ran his rapier through the heart of his own man. The fellow twisted up a startled face which immediately lost all expression. His elbow slipped out from under him and his head hit the floor with a hollow thump.

"I don't approve," said the Fiddler softly, "of unnecessary abuse of women."

The Spider, crouched behind the corner of the wall, shut his lips grimly and lifted his automatic. The man was gallant where women were concerned, but that was no affair of the Spider. The man was also a fiendishly clever criminal who had murdered scores of persons, had looted the city until it had been driven to the verge of panic and bankruptcy. That was the affair of the Spider. He had sworn to kill this man and he would do it.

Thus Wentworth goaded himself, but his inner being countered with the fact that the Fiddler had once spared the Spider's life, had saved two women from dishonor. There seemed to be a physical inability to pull the trigger of the leveled automatic.

So be it, then.

He thrust the rapier through the edge of his cape, palmed both automatics and stepped out into the hall. Then he let his mocking laughter ring out.

"Turn, fools and fight!" he challenged. "The Spider is here."

The three minions of the Fiddler whirled as if they were one mechanism, yet Wentworth cursed furiously, between clenched teeth, as he saw that the Fiddler had no intention of whirling thus to join the battle.

While the man turned slowly about, Wentworth's weapons spoke a spiteful epic of death, filling the hall with thunder. Three shots sped from his automatics and three men crashed down to the floor, each with a bullet through his forehead.

And still the Fiddler had not faced entirely about, still he made no move to draw his weapon. He held his rapier, point down, in his right hand and from its gleaming point red blood dripped slowly. A casual smile crossed his lips and Wentworth recognized with a start of amazement who it was the man caricatured, who it was that the Fiddler must be intending to murder at eleven-thirty the following Thursday night. The disguise was that of the Governor of New York!

The recognition thinned Wentworth's lips. Truly this man

chose his victims in high places. And with the man still making no effort to draw a gun, only standing there rapier in hand, Wentworth dropped his own automatics into his pockets—with a curse—and whipped up his rapier in salute.

Abruptly the ballroom doors flung wide. Four men, grasping revolvers, crouched in the entrance. Too late, Wentworth saw that he had been tricked into a position from which there was no escape. The Fiddler now could have him shot down… The Spider poised his rapier, prepared to make one last effort to triumph.

"Don't shoot," the Fiddler ordered his men in a casual voice. "I have an idea I am being challenged to a duel of rapiers."

Gracefully he swept his own blade to salute, and the two prospective combatants stood stiffly. Both their rapiers had tasted blood this night; the brilliance of their points was dimmed. Death was in the eyes of both as they stood, very nearly of a size, well proportioned as to shoulders, slender in the hips, and awaited a signal. Their gaze met unwaveringly and on the lips of both were tight, hard smiles.

"*En gardé!*" Wentworth cried.

The rapiers whistled down and both men crouched, left hands lifted on balance, weapons circling almost at arm's length. The Spider danced in, lunging strongly, recovering with lightning rapidity—yet not a moment too soon. He barely turned the Fiddler's riposte from his throat.

"Bravo!" he cried.

THE FIDDLER'S lips curved, but the light in his eyes was hard and bitter. He thrust swiftly, recovered, and lunged.

Wentworth was forced to break ground, the Fiddler held what he had gained. But the Spider knew now what he had wanted to learn: the length of the other's lunge. It was formidable, but his own was better.

The Fiddler sprang back a full two feet from the out-licking point of a thrust and Wentworth lunged instantly. His lunge was almost acrobatic. His feet quit the floor, the left trailing behind, the right drawn under him. His entire body was stretched out, a prolonged turn of the rapier. The Fiddler sprang back, tried wildly for a parry that would have impaled Wentworth on the impetus of his own attack had it succeeded.

But the Spider's powerfully driven blade knocked aside the other's and struck true toward the Fiddler's heart. The criminal reeled back, his blade dropping. Wentworth recovered, a puzzled frown on his forehead. He had struck true, yet the blade had not had the feel of penetrating.

It was as if he had struck something yielding yet solid. Not a steel vest....

Swift movement, on his right pulled Wentworth's eyes that way. He caught a glimpse of Jerry, hurling a chair. Even as he spotted the heavy chair flying at him, it was too late to duck. He whipped up the point of his rapier. There was a crunch as the point ate home. The blade bent, snapped, and the chair crashed on. Its back caught Wentworth over the head and spilled him to the floor. In the moment before the blow wiped out consciousness, the Spider's thoughts were all black. He was doomed, whether the Fiddler carried him away or police won their way through.

CHAPTER 12
THE FIDDLER PLANS ANEW

A VOICE was calling to Wentworth from a great distance and he couldn't quite make out the words. He strained and strained to hear, and finally, blurrily, recognized his own name. He tried to answer and abruptly, with a snap inside his brain, he was conscious.

"Quick, Dick," Nita's voice was frantic. "Quick. I can't drag you any further and the police know you're missing."

Wentworth pulled himself groggily to his feet, fighting the pain in his brain. Even before he understood what was happening, he was struggling along with Nita's arm half supporting him. The action and the pain rapidly completed the work of restoration. He glanced about, found they were hurrying along a corridor of the hotel. Behind him were shouts and excitement.

"What happened?" he asked heavily.

"The Fiddler and his men got away," she told him. "They threw a bomb down the elevator shaft and one down the stairways, blocked them both, and then finished robbing the people. When the police came up on firemen's ladders, they ran upward into the hotel and simply disappeared."

Wentworth grunted. They were climbing a flight of stairs now toward the next floor and the cries of police were fainter behind them. He frowned, looked down at the floor. "Do you know whether Kirk was…."

Nita shook her head. "They carried him away in an ambulance. He's in bad shape, I'm afraid."

It was late in the morning before he was away from the hotel, with Nita, and racing to the hospital where Kirkpatrick had been taken. The surgeon, Doctor Devoe, was leaving the building as they drove up and Wentworth, knowing he was the chief of staff of the hospital, stopped him on the sidewalk.

"Kirkpatrick?" Wentworth said eagerly.

Devoe's eyes were weary. He shook his head slowly.

"I don't know," he said. "The bullet missed the spine and kidneys, missed every vital organ by some miracle, but it perforated the intestines in six places. I removed the punctures...." A tired smile crossed his lips. "The operation was a success."

Wentworth knew the rest of the phrase and it tightened an iron band about his heart. "The operation was a success, but the patient died." A jest it was. But, Good God, this was Kirkpatrick! This was his friend!

"In heaven's name, Doctor Devoe," Wentworth said hoarsely, "if there is anything... money's no object."

The doctor nodded gravely. "Everything that can be done has been done," he said. "Luckily, he didn't lose too much blood externally... Internal hemorrhage of course."

WENTWORTH WAS doomed to inaction. He discovered where Tony Musette worked behind a counter at Macy's, and Nita used her influence to get a job in the same department. Richard Wentworth disappeared and Limpy Magee returned to his shop off the Bowery.

Days grew into a week without any new happenings except that, with the removal of Kirkpatrick from the office of Commissioner and the retirement and dismissal of many of his leading officials, the police defense had become sadly weakened. Fewer of them were killed by bandits, but that was because they lacked the incentive to pursue the fleeing killers' cars.

Kirkpatrick still hovered between life and death. Once there was a slight improvement reported and Wentworth rejoiced, but two days later his friend slipped back again. He had never been off the danger list and Dr. Devoe, with matchless, untiring devotion, was fighting peritonitis and pneumonia, both of which threatened the patient in his weakened condition.

Then the Governor, ringed about with guards, was killed by a knife either thrown or shot through a window, and the Death Fiddler came boastfully into Collins' in the garb of his victim! Wentworth, as Limpy Magee, arrived minutes after the Fiddler left and despair nearly overwhelmed him.

For hours, for days he had been awaiting another opportunity to face the Fiddler. And here he had missed one of the leader's rare appearances. Now he sat slumped forward over his table, hands shoved into the tousled mop of his hair.

As on his every visit, Snakey Annie sauntered up and dropped into a chair across from him.

A cigarette dangled from her lip, and her eyes were black and brilliant as she leaned forward, sifting smoke out of her nostrils.

"Why the weeps, big boy?" Her voice was softly insinuating. "Ain't I with you?"

Wentworth jerked up, staring at her with the venomous, blood-shot eyes that were part of his disguise. "Scram, will you," he snarled. "I'm sick of looking at your ugly mug."

Snakey Annie's lips quirked upward at the left corner. "Tell me more, Limpy, I love it." She slid her elbows on the table, rested chin on fists. She seemed not to be speaking now, but words breathed from her motionless lips.

"Limpy, if you're wise, you'll play along with me," she said.

Wentworth continued to stare at her. Then he caught up his whisky glass and tossed the vile liquor against his pallet, throwing back his head. He wiped the back of his hand across his mouth.

"All right, spill it," he snarled.

Snakey Annie inhaled deeply of her cigarette, eyes nearly closed. Her lips twisted again in a smile and she pushed up from the chair, then thrust her head at him as viciously as the reptile whose name she bore.

"Go to hell!" she spat at him. "I know people who will *pay* for what I know."

Wentworth tried to hide the calculation that crept into his eyes as he leered up at her.

"Scram!" he snarled again. Lurching to his feet he slapped viciously at her. She dodged and sauntered away with an exaggerated swaying of her hips. Wentworth settled back into his chair as if too drunk to do anything else. He dropped his head on his crossed arms and no one bothered him. Limpy Magee was one of the elite.

BUT HIS mind was totally unfogged with liquor. The hint from the girl had swept his brain clean of worry and fatigue, wiped out in a few words the despair that had gripped him. What had she hinted? Did she mean she had discovered that he was in disguise? Or was it merely that she had private information which she thought valuable? No way of telling, of course, unless he went after her.

A tight smile twisted his lips, hidden by his folded arms. That wouldn't be necessary. Snakey Annie would come back again. He felt the table shift under his weight and some one dropped into the opposite chair. A thin, whining voice prodded at him.

"Wake up, Limpy," it urged, "I got big news for youse."

Wentworth stirred grumpily, cursed and ordered the speaker away. He knew who it was. Danny Dawson had been a shadow for him at every appearance in the back room of Collins' place. The little yegg seemed to look upon Limpy Magee as little short of a god. Indeed, it was a rare thing that one crook would risk his life to save another when police were at his heels, and Limpy had been scarcely an acquaintance to Danny when he had done that.

Danny's whining voice persisted and finally Wentworth sat up, blearily awake. The little yegg leaned confidentially across the table, his narrow, horse-nosed face grinning slyly beneath a foppish white felt.

"I ain't supposed to tell youse till five a.m.," he said, "but I'll break a rule for a pard any day. Youse is going to see you-know-who in the a.m."

Wentworth peered with apparent dullness at Danny's shrewd face, but his heart sprang up into his throat and beat there like a great thudding drum. He was to see the Fiddler again!

"What the hell y'talkin' about?" he demanded. Danny flung a look over his shoulder to see that nobody was near and the smile stayed on his face. "The Fiddler," he whispered. "He wants youse to come see him again."

Wentworth frowned, shrugged his shoulders. "So what?"

His indifference seemed to frighten Danny.

"I ain't goin' to talk about what I said no more until five a.m.," he said. "What's the matter wit' youse and Annie? She's been givin' me the glad-eye since I palled up wit' youse and tonight she looked like she was wantin' to knife me. What's the matter?"

Wentworth looked owlishly at Danny, shook his head and signaled for drinks. It was only eleven o'clock. He had hours to wait before he could come face to face again with the Fiddler. His mind shifted to Snakey Annie, and he forced himself to study the possible meaning of her words. But he merely shrugged at Danny's inquiries, and both fell to drinking silently.

DESPITE HIS relaxed look, Wentworth was tense with apprehension. If Annie had been about Limpy Magee's shop spying on him and had seen something to make her suspicious… Good Lord, he couldn't let her betray him now, not when he was within hours of meeting finally the dread criminal genius who ruled the city! He must get hold of her and learn her secret.

"Listen," said Danny, breaking a long, restless silence, "youse don't want to treat Annie too rough. There ain't nothin' she won't do, get her riled. Want I should take a walk over…" He eased to his feet.

"Sit down!" Wentworth snapped. He rolled his head limply on his neck and looked about him. A buxom blonde in a vivid green sweater and checked skirt was sauntering by with much swaying of hips and Wentworth reached out and hooked her about the waist.

"Come'n see papa, baby," he grinned.

The blonde spun about, green-eyed with anger until she recognized Limpy, then she grinned, sliding a hand over his mouse-colored hair, behind his head.

"How're yuh, Limpy? What's the idea insultin' a poor woiking goil?"

Wentworth guffawed loudly, hauled the girl—Jessie James, she called herself—down on his knee. She was flattered at attention from the famous Limpy Magee, and put an affectionate arm about his shoulders. That lasted about thirty seconds. Snakey Annie blew up in a whirlwind as Wentworth had known she would and Jessie James took to her heels squealing, trying to stretch her tight checkered skirt into a space-covering stride.

Then Annie was standing before Wentworth with her hands set on her silk-covered hips, glowering down at him.

"You're just hell on claim-jumpers, ain't you, baby?" Wentworth chuckled at her. He reached out and caught Annie's left wrist. She fought wildly, but the Spider's lithe strength was too much. Without apparent effort, he pulled her toward him and plumped her on his lap with her hands locked behind.

She kicked at him viciously, but without effect, and finally, amid the laughter of the entire room, sat quite still upon Wentworth's good right knee, his left being stretched out stiffly, propped on a chair.

"What's the matter, Annie?" Wentworth jeered at her. "This is where you've been wanting to get for ages. Now what's eatin' you?"

Annie's black eyes were just on a level with his, even though she sat in his lap. They burned with hate and baffled anger.

Her hands were pinioned behind her with Wentworth's left. His right arm, clamped across her thighs, held her immovable. Abruptly he caught her chin with his right hand and kissed her very thoroughly.

Danny had left the table and the others in the room were attending to their own business now. The fight had been a novelty, but public flirting wasn't. Wentworth felt traitorous in what he did, but he had made greater sacrifices.

With that fierce kiss upon her lips, Snaky Annie went suddenly limp in his arms. She no longer fought nor sat stiffly erect upon his knees. He released her wrists and her arms closed about his neck.

"Why you been so mean to me, Limpy?" she whispered against her ear.

WENTWORTH LAUGHED shortly. The bitterness in it was not feigned. Duty bade him love this girl, while the woman who held his heart was ever denied him by the stern path of his service to humanity. They could not even work side by side when they fought a common danger, lest her very nearness to the Spider doom her horribly at the hands of his enemies. Yet this little trollop of the Underworld, as ready with her kisses as her gun, a girl not long out of her teens who was reported—truthfully, Wentworth knew—to have killed two men in a holdup, was his for the asking. He did not even need to ask. No wonder his laughter was bitter!

But Snakey Annie, her hard eyes softened now, did not question the quality of his mirth. She laughed too, and snuggled against his chest, curling her feet up under her. Her black hair was a cloud before his face and he found that the fragrance of the hair of a woman who has killed is as sweet as any other's. She seemed to bear no rancor that he had spurned her so long. She cared only that at last she was in his arms.

Apparently, she had settled for a long stay. But that was not Wentworth's plan. There was certain information he wanted from her, the news with which she had threatened him. Since she did not volunteer, he must find other means without asking her. A question would be fatal.

"Get up," he growled, "you're breaking my game leg."

He shoved her roughly erect and she almost fell in scrambling to her feet. But nothing seemed to annoy her now. She pulled a chair close and sat looking at him through the smoke of a newly lighted cigarette. Wentworth ignored her, gazed deliberately past her inviting face to the noisy crowd about other tables, to be seen dimly through the fog of smoke. Ten minutes of that and Annie jumped to her feet.

"Come on," she said, catching Wentworth by the arm, "let's get out of here."

Wentworth looked up at her sourly, shrugged loose of her grip. "Run along and play," he growled.

Annie urged him, winked voluptuous promises, smiled and made inviting *moues,* but Wentworth was indifferent to all. Finally she bent close to his ear, nipped it with her teeth.

"Don't you want to know what I know?" she whispered.

Wentworth laughed nastily. "I've forgotten more than you know, or ever will."

Wentworth struck the head of the Death Fiddler with the hilt of his knife.

"Yeah?" she glowered down at him. "Maybe you know then that the Metropolitan is going to be robbed in the morning."

"What?"

She was pleased at the startled exclamation, at his quick glance into her face. She smiled, bent close, brushed his face with her dangling hair.

"They're going to rob the Metropolitan Art Museum in the morning," she murmured. "Come on, and I'll tell you all about it."

Wentworth lurched heavily to his feet, caught up his greasy cap from the next chair and looked sullenly about the room. Those at the nearest tables turned and waved a farewell, but Wentworth saw none of that. He saw only the picture that Snakey Annie's words had raised before his startled eyes. The Metropolitan Art Museum, the treasures of the centuries, looted by the Death Fiddler. And the girl knew the details. He would have to learn them at all costs, and defeat the criminal hordes.

Danny swaggered close. "Don't forget I want to see youse at five a.m.," he sniggered.

"Come over to the shop," Wentworth grunted. He shoved his fists into his pockets and limped toward the door. Snakey Annie hung onto his left, lolling her head against him. She didn't even mind when he shouldered it roughly away.

The Metropolitan! Wentworth drew in a slow, noisy breath, then hissed it out between his teeth. This was one crime they would not get away with. He grinned suddenly. It was possible that the Fiddler would not be there to participate, after the Spider paid him a visit!

CHAPTER 13
LIMPY MAGEE IS UNMASKED

WENTWORTH WAS waiting in front of Limpy Magee's shop at a little before five o'clock when Danny came swaggering down the street for him. There was a brisk chill in the pre-dawn air, and mist lay heavy over the river. Against the softly purple sky, buildings stood squat and black.

Danny was chipper. He clapped Wentworth on his hunched shoulders and proclaimed that it was a fine morning.

"A hell of a time this guy picks for interviews," Wentworth growled. "A hell of a time."

They took a taxi directly to the west side, crossed Fifth Avenue and circled back on Tenth Street, where they went into a basement areaway. Wentworth limped in first when the grating was opened, this time by a butler without bullet wounds. Danny pushed forward, but the grating slammed in his face.

"The Master says you've finished for tonight," the butler said.

It was with a sense of utter loss that Wentworth saw Danny's narrow, swaggering shoulders disappear. It seemed ominous that this time he should be separated from the little yegg. It was not impossible, either, that the Fiddler had discovered that Patrolman Bill Horace was still alive. Wentworth had not seen the policeman since handing him Kirkpatrick's message.

"This way, sir," said the butler.

Wentworth braced himself instinctively, unbuttoned his coat so that his guns would be ready to hand, then stumped along a narrow, badly lighted hall, into a room at its end.

Once more the bodies of the past victims, in effigy, were sprawled on tables along the wall. Governor Ham was there with the knife in his heart, and Judge Scott with his bullet-pocked shirt. The ceiling was low and from a beam against the far side, a figure had been hanged. There before a five-foot fireplace lay a naked man, his feet so close to the coals that… that… Wentworth cursed under his breath. It must be in his imagination that he smelled seared human flesh. He limped across to the fireplace, held his hands to the blaze—then stiffened, horror and anger alike quivering through his body.

That figure whose feet scorched in the fire was actually a man! That is, it had been a man, though it was only cold clay now. Traced upon the chest in elaborate detail was a huge violin.

Nausea hit him like a blow as he jerked his eyes away from that pitiful body on the floor. He remembered now where he had seen that man who lay so terribly dead by the fire.

Last night that man had been… *had been with Snakey Annie!* WENTWORTH'S LIPS tightened grimly. Was that why he had been brought here? Was this man dead because he had babbled to Snakey Annie about the pending Metropolitan robbery? If so, his own turn might well come next. He was glad he had his guns.

Slowly Wentworth forced himself to calmness. With his eyes he searched the room, which was lighted only by the glimmer from the fire. There was nothing here save the table with the effigies of murder, and that body before the fire which was not an effigy. The far wall, the back of the room, seemed solid.

But even as his eyes surveyed it, a slit of greenish light split it from top to bottom. Majestically that slit widened, the two halves of the wall collapsed to either side and in a downward shaft of the ghastly light the Death Fiddler was revealed.

Wentworth felt his muscles jerk with surprise as he realized the disguise the Fiddler wore. He controlled himself with a frantic effort. Limpy Magee should not indicate that he knew this man, though. Wentworth's recognition of him sent the blood humming through his veins in anger. The Fiddler was disguised as Dodson Larrimore, the secretary to the Mayor! Between his eyes was a red-blue bullet hole.

"I am glad," said the Fiddler softly, "that you were amused by last night's entertainment."

It was Limpy Magee who answered, stammering, "Cheez, chief, I ain't done nothing."

The Fiddler's face remained expressionless as his gentle voice asked: "Are you sure?" He laughed at Limpy Magee's trembling reassurance, and went on. "I didn't bring you here for punishment, Limpy. I brought you here to ask a favor—a favor for which I am willing to pay well."

"What d'you want me to do, chief?" he asked with feigned eagerness.

The Fiddler laughed once more. "A very simple thing. I want you to pay a visit which I've promised this coming Thursday night at eleven-thirty."

Wentworth stood motionless while the full import of the man's words stabbed into his brain. The Fiddler had chosen him to make this week's kill!

And the man he had selected to die was Kirkpatrick's friend, the man who had been supplying him with police information—Dodson Larrimore!

"I want you to blast the Mayor's secretary for me," the Fiddler was saying. "You'll be given any help you want, either in getting into a position to shoot, or in escaping afterward. In cases where the victims are forewarned, I make a point of planning the kills myself. But I think you are a man of ingenuity, Limpy. I shall leave this entirely in your hands."

WENTWORTH MOVED forward a few halting feet. He was wondering desperately how he could kill this man. Bullets had failed once before. The effigy of the Governor lay on Wentworth's right, dagger in his chest. Perhaps a knife thrust into the Fiddler's neck would succeed….

He was beside the body of the Governor now. He looked at it, and back to the Fiddler with admiring eyes.

"Cheez, nobody's too big for you, are they, chief? The Governor gets in your way and, bingo, he's gone. What's the Mayor's secretary done to you, chief?"

"I prefer men who don't ask questions," said the Fiddler coldly. "You will be told where to come for your reward when you have killed Larrimore."

As he finished speaking, the collapsible walls began to slide together before him. The Spider's breath hissed out. It was now or never. Without warning or sound, he snatched the knife from the breast of the Governor's effigy and sprang toward the Death Fiddler. He just managed to squeeze through before the walls closed behind him, then he flung himself toward the other. The man did not move, his features did not change, as Wentworth leaped.

Wentworth's left hand pinioned down the arms. He presented the point of the knife to the Fiddler's throat. He was nerving himself to thrust, to remove this murderer of the great, the man who terrorized the entire city. His jaw clenched. He hunched his shoulders to drive the blade home… and realized that the wrists beneath his left hand were cold. That they did not yield to his pressure as would normal flesh.

With an oath, Wentworth reversed the knife and struck the head with its hilt. The head tottered, rolled from the Death Fiddler's shoulders, and thudded to the floor. A thin red liquid seeped out from the spot where it had rested, and Wentworth, laughing crazily, savagely sprawled the whole carcass to the floor. The body, like the head, like those effigies against the wall, was made of wax!

The red fluid was between the outer layer of wax and the *papier-mâché* form on which it was molded. Furiously, Wentworth mauled the figure, prying out its secrets. He found two thin wires running from the body backward toward the wall. He knew the answer now. A loud-speaker arrangement had spoken for the waxen figure. Its movements in the previous interview had been stiff and mechanical, as he remembered them—because of some type of geared machinery within the wax figure, no doubt. Either that or invisibly fine black threads lifting the limbs like some ghastly marionette. And one other thing—the Death Fiddler could see into the room! That meant he was within reach.

WITH A sharp laugh, Wentworth swept the green lamp to the floor and smashed it. In utter darkness, he searched ceiling and wall with alert eyes. No gleam of light betrayed a peephole. But without warning the entire back wall of the room folded in upon itself to the sides. Only dim gray light came in but it revealed five men who stood waiting. As soon as the wall opened the way, they began shooting, fanning the darkness with a close net of lead.

Behind them, over their heads, a searchlight blazed out, deluging the room with brilliant illumination, veiling the men with its dazzle. Wentworth's first shot smashed that and with two more shots he dropped two men. He was crouched behind the chair where the wax figure of the Fiddler had sat, but he soon found it offered no protection. Bullets splintered through it and whined close by his head. The searchlight, brief as had been its flash, had betrayed the Spider's hiding place.

Flinging flat on the floor, he wriggled toward the wax figure. He was in a dark cavern while others were outlined against the sickly gray light creeping in through ground-level windows. The sun had risen, though in this canyon of brick walls it was still pre-dawn dusk. However, it was enough to silhouette the gang-sters, and Wentworth picked them off, one by one.

Wentworth drew a deep slow breath, a lungful of cordite fumes which made him cough. No one fired at the sound, and he nodded to himself. His victory seemed complete. But he reloaded his guns before he got cautiously to his feet and flung the beam of a pocket flash over the shambles he had created.

Swiftly he went from victim to victim, pressing his dread seal to the foreheads of the dead, searching each face hopefully. As he came to the last, he cursed in anger. The Death Fiddler was not among them. Not that he knew the man's face, but he did know that none of these who had died had the intelligence of the Fiddler.

He sprang to the back of the room and found a courtyard, tightly encased by walls of brick. Climbing out, he caught the sill of a first story window above and drew himself up slowly. The apartment overhead was empty and he smashed that window with his gun butt while dangling with one arm on the sill. Then he scrambled inside.

He was in a large room, which duplicated the one below. Upon a table rested a microphone. Two levers were fastened to the floor, and overhead ran the ropes of counterbalanced weights which evidently had operated the walls below. A periscope pierced the floor. This, then, was where the Death Fiddler operated.

FOR A man who had just wiped out a group of formidable enemies, the Spider was strangely morose as he limped northward beneath the elevated railway structure. His thoughts were dark, and with reason. All the information he had gained concerning the Fiddler he had learned while posing as Limpy Magee. Now he must abandon that personality.

He made a wry face. He had already called the new Commissioner of Police, Flynn, and as the Spider had warned him against the robbery of the Metropolitan Museum today by men who would wear the uniforms of guards and take the places of the regular men.

"Impossible," Flynn had spluttered, "and let me tell you something, Mr. Spider. If you're wise, you'll leave this town. I'm going to run you to earth if it's the last thing I do."

He had tried to persuade Flynn that he spoke the truth, but he had not succeeded. The curator of the museum had been equally dubious. Larrimore, when called, had been unable to convince the Mayor. It seemed that, with Kirkpatrick out of office, all sanity and intelligence had deserted the directors of the city's destiny. So that now the task of guarding the stupendous treasures of the Museum rested in Wentworth's hands and his alone.

Two hours would elapse, Wentworth figured—glancing at a clock in a barber shop—before the change of guards at the Metropolitan took place; and it would not be until a while later that the treasures would be taken. Deciding, therefore, to visit his home first, he stepped into a convenient drugstore and called Ram Singh, directing the Hindu to meet him with the Lancia. Twenty minutes later, within its curtained rear, he abandoned the identity of Limpy Magee and became, once more, Richard Wentworth.

As the Lancia slid along, there was an unaccustomed slump to his shoulders. His heart seemed oppressed by leaden weights. The disaster that had followed him in recent crusades against the Underworld seemed to have found him again. Gloomily he recalled how, not so long ago, he had narrowly escaped death, first at the hands of a shrewd opponent, then at the hands of police when his faithful chauffeur and former sergeant, Jackson, had sacrificed himself. Jackson had taken the bullet intended for the Spider and afterwards had confessed all the Spider's crimes, taking the blame upon himself. The nation had paid homage at his funeral. Even the government had joined.

It had saved Wentworth, but he had lost a faithful servitor, a tried and true friend who had helped him through many a savage battle. Now, it seemed, he was in a fair way to losing another.

He phoned the hospital directly on returning to his apartment, and learned that Kirkpatrick had spent another restless night. Dr. Devoe, his voice somber, announced that they were using an oxygen tent now. When they reached that stage... And he was responsible for Kirkpatrick's approaching death, Wentworth told himself bitterly! If he had warned his friend, Kirkpatrick might have been prepared for a fight.

And then there was Nita. Nita, brave and uncomplaining, who had suffered the tortures of the damned to help him in his work. He must phone Nita....

Her voice was fresh and cheerful. "It's all right being a shop girl," she said. "I get a lot of fun out of it, but that's because I know that any night I wish I can step out to Delmonico's or Pierre's for dinner and get something really superlative in the line of food or wines."

"An excellent idea." Wentworth could never help being stirred by the mere thought of her presence. "Excellent. This is Monday, shall we say Thursday night? Delmonico's?"

"Dick!" Nita's voice was rich with hope. "Dick, do you mean...."

His laughter was bitter. "No, I don't mean the fight is over. I mean only that Limpy Magee is dead and that, barring accidents, there is no need to deprive ourselves of a good meal now and then."

Nita detected the undertones of his voice. "I'm relieved," she said. "I was afraid Limpy was going to harm you one of these days. Tony Musette hates him terribly. She told me yesterday how Limpy killed her brother and she said that her boy friend was going to see that he paid for it. She said that Limpy was under the protection of a certain criminal and that Jerry—the boy friend—didn't dare do anything about it until he could undermine Limpy's connections. She seemed to think that the process was well under way."

Wentworth questioned her quickly, but Nita knew no details and interrupted with a laugh.

"See you Thursday, Dick, if not before. Meantime, the poor working girl has to hurry to work or she'll be docked for being late."

Wentworth was prepared to leave at once for the Metropolitan, but old Jenkyns insisted on serving breakfast, whereupon he found that he had an appetite.

The papers were laid before him. On top an extra blazed with the news of five more kills by the Spider. The mechanical tricks of the house were shown with artist's drawings. There was a picture also of a taxi driver who, it was alleged, had delivered a man who limped to the door where the shambles had been discovered.

Wentworth saw that this edition was a "third extra." The police had worked fast, all right. The chances were that they had already identified either the "man who limped" or Danny Dawson. If not, they soon would have the information.

Wentworth smiled thinly. Well, the Spider was known in two characters now; as Limpy Magee and as the hunchbacked Tito Caliepi, whose original name already was forgotten. To everyone that hunchbacked, sinister figure in cape and broad hat was not Tito, but the Spider. It might soon be that way with Limpy Magee.

Wentworth finished his breakfast and left, with Ram Singh following respectfully. In the Lancia once more, Wentworth spoke at length through the tube to his faithful Hindu.

"I shall make no attempt to prevent the robbery of the Metropolitan," he said slowly. "They are too many for us and it would only invite disaster. What I plan is this: When the last of the treasure trucks—there will have to be at least four, I should say—gets under way, I intend to board it and either capture or kill the men upon it. I shall then disguise myself as one of the men and follow the other trucks to whatever hiding place has been selected.

"My purpose is to discover the hideout of the Death Fiddler and if possible destroy him. I tell you this, Ram Singh, so that you will understand your part. You are to follow in the Lancia when I take over the truck, bringing me the necessary make-up materials and afterwards carrying away the prisoners—if any."

Wentworth could find no loophole in his plan, but he felt a strange fatalism about the coming engagement with the Death Fiddler and his men. Many times he had attempted even more daring invasions of an enemy camp, and came away successfully.

His keen brain and alertly responsive muscles had always carried him to safety. But a strangely hostile destiny followed him these days… in which, it seemed, there were no loopholes.

No loopholes! He laughed sharply. There was always the loophole of death.

CHAPTER 14
THE RACE AGAINST DEATH

T HE LANCIA purred softly in weaving its way north-ward through the early morning traffic of Fifth Avenue. The day had lost its earlier crisp freshness; there was a hint of rain now in the haze of blue sky. Wentworth saw these things without realization, for his depression had returned with increased strength.

Ram Singh swung around and drew up before the Metropol-itan Museum. Wentworth glanced at his watch. It was a fearful commentary on the fear engendered by the Death Fiddler, that the Lancia had made the run straight up Fifth Avenue at its most crowded hour in something under fifteen minutes!

Wentworth made no effort at disguise. He did not intend at this time to take any action against the minions of the Fiddler. He was chiefly interested at present in looking over the scene.

He saw a huge furniture van lurch over the curb and crawl along the concrete drive which circled to the back of the long, low, museum building. There were five men upon its broad seat. Wentworth's lips twisted crookedly. The odds against him were greater than he had thought. Single-handed, he must capture a truck guarded by five men.

Within the museum, the door of which was watched by two men in gray uniforms, he found a dozen men busy in one room. He started to enter, but another uniformed guard turned him politely aside.

"If you don't mind, sir, don't go in there," he said. "A borrowed collection is being taken back to its owner."

Wentworth nodded casually, then strolled on through the big chambers. He was conscious that the guard's eyes followed him suspiciously, but he was determined to learn the extent of the depredations. No one except a casual visitor here and there, the guards, and the men in that one room, were in evidence.

Wentworth nodded as he realized the full cleverness of the plan. All these rooms were closed on some occasions—for cleaning, or rearrangement of exhibits. When the band had finished with that one room, they undoubtedly would close it and place one of the regular signs on the door. After that, they would proceed to the next room to be looted. It was unlikely that any visitor would remain long enough to become suspicious. And if anyone did call a policeman, undoubtedly the moving men would produce an order signed by at least the assistant curator....

Kirkpatrick would soon have broken up this smooth theft, Wentworth knew. But Flynn would only grow red in the face and deliver another ultimatum if Wentworth called. The man was honest enough but he could not seem to visualize the extent to which modern criminals would go.

Back in the Lancia, Wentworth sped southward again. Entering Central Park, he directed Ram Singh to find a place where parking was permitted. Then he alighted and climbed a rise, thickly grown with shrubbery, where he could watch without interruption. Only one thing worried him. It was said that the Fiddler always directed his men in person, but there had been no one in the museum who might in any way have been identified as the Fiddler.

BY NOON the sky was completely overcast; a little before two o'clock a misting rain began to fall. It fogged Wentworth's vision and he left his cover to move closer. From the speed at which the looters worked, he believed that the last truck would be ready to leave within the next hour. The Spider must be ready then to act.

One truck already had departed; that one had headed north along Fifth Avenue, so that Wentworth had had the Lancia parked on that side of the museum. Then, with Ram Singh waiting in the car near an apartment house, as were a half dozen other chauffeurs, Wentworth himself strolled slowly up the avenue. He was a bit conspicuous in the drizzle, but he would have to take his chances on that.

He had reached Ninety-second Street when the heavy truck from the museum lumbered past. A half block behind trailed a sedan carrying four men, obviously gunmen. The Lancia swerved to the curb immediately afterward, Wentworth jumped in, and they began the tedious work of trailing.

In the back, Wentworth opened his wardrobe and quickly resumed the garb of Limpy Magee. He was already proscribed; it mattered little what further offenses against the Fiddler he committed. He opened a small window on the right side, and signaled to Ram Singh to overtake the gangster car.

The rain grew heavier and small cold drops shot against his face as he waited tensely by the open window. He had expected this convoy car, and he was prepared to eliminate it.

"Better make them speed up a little before you pass," he told Ram Singh through the tube. He saw the Hindu's turbaned head nod understanding, then the Lancia began to pass traffic with a quiet, effortless speed. A boy in a Ford sedan tried to squeeze out ahead from the right hand lane, but Ram Singh out-bluffed him with an extra notch of speed. The boy fell back, shouting vigorous curses.

ANOTHER BLOCK and the Lancia's nose was just behind the Cadillac in which the gunmen rode. With the truculence which characterized such individuals, their car was squarely in the center of the lane so that cars could pass neither to right nor left.

Ram Singh touched the trumpet horn to a polite, questioning note. The car ahead did not change position. Ram Singh held the horn down and Wentworth smiled grimly at its persistent trumpeting.

Through the rain-blurred windshield he saw the white blob of a face at the Cadillac's back-window. The horn kept on and the car ahead began to pick up a little speed. Ram Singh shoved the Lancia's nose up to its left, still sounding the horn. The Cadillac pulled ahead, its passengers glaring out angrily. The driver cranked down his window and shouted.

"Now," Wentworth said calmly.

With an effortless ease which made the other car appear to stand still, the Lancia's one hundred and seventy-five horse-power motor shot it past the sedan. And as Wentworth's open window whipped opposite that of the driver, the Spider grinned impudently and tossed a glass bomb of tear gas straight past the man's head into the Cadillac.

"Faster," he ordered. The Lancia surged forward and he cranked shut the window, peering back through the bulletproof glass in the rear. The Cadillac swerved once, twice, yawed wildly toward the southbound traffic, then its brakes gripped and the rear swung about to the right. A limousine leaped forward out of its path as, still skidding, it swung almost lazily across Fifth Avenue. On its second turn the rear end slapped the front of a double-decker bus. The Cadillac shimmied back two feet from the collision and remained stationary. Its doors were flung open on both sides and four men, hands pressed to their eyes, arms before their faces, ran wildly out and away.

One crashed blindly into the front of a second bus and disappeared under its wheels. Another tripped over a curbing and sprawled headfirst against the stone wall circling the park. The other two vanished into the thickening traffic which backed up behind the accident.

Wentworth smiled, nodded to himself, and dropped back on the cushions.

"Just keep the truck in sight for a while," he ordered.

When the treasure truck reached Yonkers and rumbled on through its streets northward toward Albany, the Lancia drew closer. As it reached the open road beyond, Ram Singh pushed the lean, long nose of the Lancia nearer. They were less than a hundred yards behind when the right hand door of the truck opened and a man leveled a machine gun along its side. Ram Singh merely swerved to the left, and the man's bullets were blocked off by the truck itself.

Wentworth bent over, slid out a shallow tray from beneath the seat. In it nestled revolvers and automatics, bombs and rifles. There was a riot gun and a sub-machine gun. He selected an Enfield army rifle with a jacketed bullet, cranked down the larger right hand window and leaned outside.

Without an order Ram Singh eased to the right again. Their re-emergence caught the machine gunner unaware. Wentworth's rifle spoke once and the man's body lunged back against the truck door, then slumped so that his feet almost dragged the road. The machine gun dangled from his neck and it was apparent that it had been strapped to him, even as he had been tied to the truck.

Wentworth saw hands reach out for the machine gun and he squeezed off another shot. The hands disappeared, but not before blood spurted from one.

The truck was hurricaning down the middle of the road now, its canvas rear cover snapping and popping in the wind, the dead man and his machine gun swinging wildly from the banging door. There was a hard, cold smile on Wentworth's lips. He signaled Ram Singh to the left and shot the rear vision mirror off the truck's mud-guard.

"Pass them on the right," he said.

IMPERTURBABLY, RAM SINGH tooled to the truck's

135

right. He did not overhaul the van rapidly, merely inched ahead. Wentworth crossed to the left of the tonneau and drew out another glass tear gas bomb. He was ready when Ram Singh suddenly spurted past the open door of the truck. As Wentworth had intended, the men were all watching the left hand side where he had shot off the mirror. The gas bomb struck the steering gear and burst, spraying gray vapor over the four men, spewing a large part of it into the driver's eyes.

The truck swayed and wobbled, rocking as it yawned from left to right. Its great speed made sudden stopping dangerous, but it also helped to clear the cabin quickly. The truck was braked perfectly. It came to a shuddering halt within thirty seconds after Wentworth's bomb had burst.

Ram Singh had slowed as soon as the Lancia was out of danger of being hit by the careening truck. The men dodged from the cabin of the truck, driven out by the tear gas, but they came shooting. One of them caught the machine gun from the man Wentworth had killed and spewed a tornado of lead at the Lancia. Wentworth calmly drilled him with his rifle, then in rapid succession picked off two more. The driver, whom Wentworth had carefully spared, turned and fled blindly when he heard his companion's guns go dead. The Lancia loafed up beside him. He emptied his automatic against its armored sides, then Wentworth leaned out and tapped him with a blackjack.

It had been a surprisingly easy victory thus far and the knowledge buoyed his spirits. He sprang from the car and, while Ram Singh once more turned about, caught up the unconscious gangster and moved at a heavy trot toward the truck. The Lancia reached the spot almost as quickly and Ram Singh tossed the bodies of the other dead into the tonneau. Then, at Wentworth's order, the Hindu raced away, took a side road half a mile ahead, and vanished.

Wentworth took time to imprint his dread seal on the dead men, then looked the truck over carefully. No bullet marks showed except on the smashed mirror. Ensconcing the unconscious man beside him, he drove on, trundling along at a thoroughly reasonable rate of speed. The motorcycle cops who presently came racing past paid him no attention at all.

The gangster revived after about five miles. Finding himself handcuffed, he first cursed Wentworth. When that had no effect he begged for information as to what was going to happen to him. His eyes were still swollen from the tear gas, and the lump on his forehead from the blackjack was an ugly blue-green.

And still Wentworth paid him no attention at all, merely keeping his own eyes on the rain-washed road ahead, through the space cleared by the sloshing windshield wiper. The beat of rain on the roof made a dreary background for the varying roar of the motor.

Presently the gangster fell silent and slumped back in his corner of the seat. Brooding upon his cuffed hands for long moments, he stared up at his captor after a while. Wentworth heard him gasp.

"Good God!" the man groaned. "You are Limpy Magee. You're… the Spider!"

NOT UNTIL then did Wentworth turn toward his prisoner—and then only to look at him with expressionless eyes.

As he swung back to watch the road again, the man made small moaning noises in his throat. After a time that stopped and he began to beg once more.

"What yuh going to do with me?" he pleaded. "For God's sake, Spider, I ain't done nothin' but steal. I ain't never killed nobody nor nothin' like that." He whimpered. "What happened to Pete and Buddy and Jack and—and Fred?" He seemed afraid to ask, and yet driven on by a fearful curiosity.

The loose lips that were part of Limpy Magee's disguise twitched into a mocking smile.

"I killed them," he said.

The man was silent after that. The big truck roared on through the darkening day; the rain beat in broken gusts as the wind whipped it across their path. Finally the prisoner spoke again, his voice rasping in a dry mouth.

"What… what are you going to do with me?"

Once more Wentworth smiled and the man choked down a cry, then on rising notes shrilled: "What are you going to do? What are you going to do… to *me*?" His last words were a whisper.

Wentworth let the noise of the rain beat in between them again before he answered. "That depends very much on you yourself." He made no pretense of imitating the voice of Limpy Magee, and the incongruity of his cultured tones with his shabby garb and leering face made what he said the more threatening.

In the words, the man must have caught a gleam of hope. He leaned forward, straining against the cuffs fastening him to the far side of the seat, thrusting his face with its opened mouth toward Wentworth, across the width of the truck.

"What do you mean?" he whispered.

"Information," the Spider laughed. "Information—*or death!*"

"I'm not going to squeal," the man said stubbornly, defiantly.

Wentworth nodded. He braked the truck to a halt at the head of a hill, climbed down deliberately and circled to the other side. He tossed the man the key to the handcuffs and covered him with an automatic.

"Unlock those and get out," he ordered.

The eyes of the two met and locked. The driver's gaze widened slowly until the whites showed completely around the irises.

"You'd shoot me down without a chance?" A trembling seized him. His voice quavered out between chattering teeth. "I'll talk! I'll talk!"

"Why wasn't the Fiddler himself on this job?" Wentworth asked.

It was not what he had intended to demand. He had planned to ask where the hideout was, where the treasure was being taken. But ever since he had failed to spot the Death Fiddler on the scene the man's absence had worried him. He had a persistent feeling that there was an important reason behind his missing the job.

The man's mouth gaped like a landed fish. He swallowed dryly before he could gulp out words "Another job."

"What?"

"He's planning to rob Penn Station tonight."

Wentworth stiffened. "Penn Station!"

The man nodded. "Yeah. Ticket offices. He says they take in a lot of dough, and it's easy to get. I was supposed to leave this truck and scoot back to town in a car to lend a hand, and...."

He broke off at Wentworth's sharp curse. Wentworth sprang back to the driver's seat, sent the truck lurching forward again, worked it laboriously about, and headed swiftly back for the city.

"What time is this robbery planned?" he asked anxiously, wrenching the careening truck around a sharp curve, fighting the bucking wheel.

"Five-thirty."

The man was watching Wentworth drive with a mixture of admiration and fear upon his face. His superb handling of the heavy van, the nicety with which he gauged its potentialities, clearly appealed to him as a driver. His fear was fading. He remembered old stories he had heard of the Spider and he remembered that the Spider kept his word. If he talked, he would not die, this strange Limpy Magee had said, and thinking of that, the driver gained new courage.

WENTWORTH'S FACE was set and hard. The clock on the dash read four-twenty-five. Not a chance in a hundred that he could make Penn Station in time in a passenger car, much less in this truck. But he had instructed Ram Singh to circle back to Dobbs Ferry and wait there until midnight for him. The Lancia would help. Grimly Wentworth decided to try once more to call police. If they had learned of the museum robbery, they might listen.

Ten minutes later, he rolled the truck to a halt before a gas station in Dobbs Ferry, spotted his Lancia at the curb, and dropped down from the seat. He went around the driver's side of the limousine and climbed into the back.

"New York," he snapped at Ram Singh. "As fast as you can make it!"

Before the Lancia, racing at breakneck speed, had scorched into the outer fringes of Yonkers, Wentworth had stripped off the disguise and was himself again. That accomplished he brought the car to a halt near a centrally located hotel which was pretty apt to be crowded. Swiftly he ordered Ram Singh to hire a taxi back to Dobbs Ferry, disguise himself, take the driver to a rooming house, and leave him a prisoner there. Afterward, the Hindu was to call local police and tell them of the loot from the museum in the truck, and where the prisoner could be located.

Wentworth tossed the last words over his shoulder as he strode toward the hotel. Slipping into a coin booth he put in a call for Commissioner Flynn at New York. For five minutes he shifted restlessly from foot to foot glanced again and again at his watch. Then the wires clicked.

"Flynn!" a voice barked.

"Spider!" Wentworth hurled back at him, his lips twisted in a thin smile. "Have you found out yet that the Metropolitan Museum has been stripped?"

Flynn's end of the wire throbbed with silence for a slow count of ten, then his voice rasped over the wire again.

"What do you know?"

Wentworth closed his eyes. Thank God one thing was going right for him at last in his battle against the Death Fiddler. Even while the thought touched his mind he was talking rapidly, telling where the treasure trucks were to be found.

"Maybe you'll believe me this time," he wound up, his disguised voice flat, faintly mocking. "Tonight at five-thirty, the Fiddler is going to rob Pennsylvania Station. I'm in Yonkers and won't be able to get there. Get the lead out of your carcass and do something this time."

Seconds later he was in the Lancia, swinging out from the curb and beginning his wild dash for New York. Flynn might act this time, yet there was no certainty of it. The man was hard-headed and stubborn. He would hate to take help from one he classed as a criminal.

THE LANCIA laid its belly to the road, and raced on and on. Miles blurred past beneath the flying wheels and other cars were vagrant flashing beams of light. Wentworth kept his horn going wildly and other machines flung out of his path. Halfway along the Broadway stretch into the city a string of red lights across the road started his foot kicking the brakes. When he grasped the purpose of the lights, he was still going forty. He slowed still more, his heart beating thunderously. Those were police who blocked the road and they were stopping every car. Automobiles were backed up for a hundred yards.

Impatiently, Wentworth coasted the motor, edging along as rapidly as possible in the slow-moving line. His heart was pounding high and hard in his throat. He realized that he had not only given Flynn his whereabouts, but had indicated that he would race for New York. Undoubtedly his own speed had been spotted by the police. He cursed softly under his breath, gaining some relief from the fact that the policemen, standing out in the rain without slickers, only glanced into each car crawling past.

Finally the car ahead was passed and the Lancia rolled forward. The cop looked at him sharply, stepped up on the running board.

"Pull over to the side," he ordered.

Wentworth made no protest. It would do no good and would merely make the officer suspicious. But there was a sinking sensation at the pit of his stomach as he said, "Certainly, but please make it as quick as possible. I'm late now for an engagement."

The policeman said nothing, but when they had reached the side of the road, he peered in.

"In a hurry back there, wasn't you?" he asked belligerently.

Wentworth admitted it was a shrug. "As I told you, I'm late for an engagement." He plunged two fingers into a vest pocket, drew out a golden courtesy shield Kirkpatrick had given him. He held in his palm and the officer frowned, then growled something under his breath.

"I don't often use it," Wentworth said gently, "but I really am in a hurry." He drew out a cigar case and proffered it.

The cop grunted, took two cigars and sniffed them. His face lighted up, and he saluted.

"Sorry to have detained you, sir." He walked heavily back to his post on the line.

Wentworth sent the Lancia forward with a lurch. *He had lost another six minutes*. But the road was fairly clear ahead, thanks to the blockade, and he bore the accelerator toward the floor.

When the needle touched eighty, he eased off. At that speed, an obstacle four blocks ahead became a suicidal danger. The least curve made the tires whistle and moan, set even the low-hung Lancia rocking on its heavy springs.

He reached the Two-hundred-twenty-fifth Street bridge five minutes after five. But the rest of the trip would be a nerve wracking grind through heavy traffic. He whirled off Broadway, took back streets until he reached Riverside Drive, then streaked down the center of the double-lane road, drawing shouts and angry glares from other motorists. Street lights popped up with a sudden white flowering in the wet dusk, made streaks along the road. His blazing headlights helped gain him right-of-way.

He spotted a motorcycle policeman in a side lane and crashed a red traffic light to reach him, showed him the badge and a twenty dollar bill. "I've got to get to Penn Station in nothing flat," he said. "Can you leave your post long enough to get me to the elevated highway?"

The money changed hands and the cop sent his motorcycle popping forward as the lights changed. He started his siren going. There was a weary smile of amusement on Wentworth's lips as he blazed along at forty-five miles an hour behind the shrieking siren, down the center of the two lanes of traffic, ignoring stop lights, sending cross-traffic drivers into frightened stalls. Nowhere in the world except New York would a simple badge have earned him this. But police here were bred in the school of favoritism. It didn't extend to criminals, but privilege in the city wore a high-silk hat and drove expensive foreign cars. The politician's friends were manifold.

AT SEVENTY-SECOND STREET, the policeman circled the traffic light standard and Wentworth swung a hand as he whirred right onto the temporary ramp of the elevated automobile express highway which, with one interruption, continued miles downtown from Seventy-second street to Canal.

Leaving the highway by a convenient ramp, he raced for the Pennsylvania Station. It lacked but five minutes of five-thirty now; it would be impossible for him to reach the place in time to be ahead of the Fiddler's attempt. He should, however, get there in time for the battle, he told himself grimly.

The hands of the big station clock stood at five thirty-two when he slammed the Lancia against the curb in a restricted parking area and raced for the entrance. As he reached the fat columns dividing the opening, he heard a rattling discharge of weapons and, staring through glass doors, saw two men in police uniform whirl about in the middle of the concourse and spill to the floor.

In two long strides he reached the door. Springing inside, he pitched to the floor as he saw a man, crouched against one of the entrance gate towers, swing the muzzle of a machine gun toward him. The concourse below was empty of the commuters who should have thronged it at this hour; he breathed a prayer of hope that his warning had been heeded by Flynn in time to prevent any loss of life among bystanders.

A torrent of lead swept over him and the glass doors behind fell in a tinkling heap. Wentworth was untouched. Flat on his stomach on the stone platform, he was protected by his enemy's lower position. Twice more bursts of lead streamed above him, and by the doors he heard a man cough. Turning, he saw an elderly police official pitch stiffly forward, the uniform cap bouncing from his gray head.

Grimly, Wentworth faced toward the machine gunner again. He squirmed forward on his stomach until a quick upward jerk of his head would give him a view of the concourse, then flung up his arm. Quick as was the action, his shot was no slower. He fired twice, then sprang erect, going down the shallow steps in long leaping strides while the machine gunner still stood poised in his death plunge.

Wentworth's eyes swept a swift arc across the far side of the great vaulted hall. A high iron fence separated waiting room from the descent to the tracks and beside two of the gateways Wentworth spotted two more machine gunners. He checked his race, snapped two quick shots at the one on his right, dropped to the steps, supporting himself on one hand, and sent his last three bullets clanging along the steel network of the gate tower behind which the man crouched.

An answering hail of bullets beat about him and he pitched prone on the steps, then rolled limply down them. His other automatic against his side, he kept his eyes on the machine gunner. He saw now why there was no crowd of commuters thronging the floor. Seven men were sprawled across the steps at the far end where they had been burned down with bullets. Their bodies apparently had served as sufficient warning.

The rolling made him slightly dizzy, but he saw the machine gunner straighten and step from behind the tower to give his victim a final burst of lead. Wentworth spread his legs wide, checked his roll, pumped bullets with the rapid, unerring accuracy for which he was famed. The man collapsed over his gun and its muzzle, pushed down toward his own feet, spewed deadly steel, which gnawed its way across them and began to eat up his legs before his fall stopped the chattering weapon.

Wentworth came to his feet limping slightly with bruises—which did not hamper his speed as he sprinted toward the doors separating this, the departure platform, from the concourse beyond, where the ticket offices were located. As he sped forward, stuffing fresh cartridges into clips, guns began to speak near the ticket offices.

The Spider dodged aside, skirting the wall as he approached the doors. There had been no time at all for thought, since he had dashed into the arena and almost into a stream of lead. But now he began to wonder where the police had been placed—if, indeed, Flynn had sent any guard to the station. He was ten feet away from the doors when he got his answer.

Behind him a whistle shrilled loudly. He jerked about—to see uniformed men pouring in through all three entrances of the departure concourse. The foremost carried machine guns. And one of them, seeing Wentworth with guns in hands, threw up his weapon and at once started firing.

CHAPTER 15
THE DEATH FIDDLER
TRAPPED

WENTWORTH SPRANG frantically for the doors, which opened by means of a photo-electric cell and a beam of light. The light helped Wentworth. It flung the doors wide and he did not have even the fractional pause a man makes when, in flight, he meets any check.

He went through in a sprawling roll and, behind him, glass crashed under a welter of bullets. From the sound at least six machine guns had poured their lead after him. A slight chill ran through his body. He rolled to the protection of a column beside the doorway and flung swift, piercing eyes about the concourse beyond.

Here, too, gangsters were posted with machine guns. But they hesitated to shoot at an armed man who was in obvious flight from the blast of police whistles, the thunder of police guns. The moment of hesitation enabled Wentworth to dart to the opposite side of the hall and into the safety of a thick-walled waiting room.

Through the windows of the ticket offices, as he sprinted past, he spotted the looters at work. And crouching now where he commanded one of the exits to the series of offices along one side of the concourse, his fingers were light and ready on his triggers. However, he was unprepared for the solid phalanx of armed men appearing suddenly in the center of the concourse, moving at a heavy trot for the exit, and carrying in the midst of their flying wedge a man who crouched low for the protection of the bodies about him.

With an oath, Wentworth opened fire. He had no doubt as to the identity of that protected man. As his bullets cut into the side of the wedge, two men stumbled down, then a third pitched over on top of them. The others closed in about the chief they guarded and in an instant were out of sight.

The last man had scarcely vanished behind the edge of the ticket offices which cut off Wentworth's view when there was a stunning blast of fire. It sounded as if a hundred machine guns had cut loose at once. The confining walls hammered back the beat and pound of the explosions. Two men appeared from around the corner where the phalanx had vanished. Before they had taken two leaping strides, bullets caught them.

One sprang into the air like a dancer, head wrenched back, arms thrown high, legs spanning in a stride. He went limp in mid-air and when he hit, his head bounced in a sickening way. The other figure arched backward as if a pile-driver had caught him in the center of the back. Teeth flew when his face smacked down.

Wentworth stepped stealthily backward. There was only one explanation of that fearful blast. Flynn had planted a machine gun battery somewhere… the plane! That was it. He had planted men in the huge Ford monoplane which had been assembled in the concourse long ago to serve as an advertisement for air travel. His men had hidden in the plane until he signaled, then stepped out or poked their guns through smashed windows, and poured that withering fire. Not a man had escaped. An exultant

150

Not a man of the phalanx escaped!
Flynn has planted machine gunners
in the advertising plane!

warmth spread through Wentworth. The Fiddler had fallen prey to other guns than the Spider's, but the means of his death did not matter....

WENTWORTH STRAIGHTENED to steal away. Since the man was dead, there was no point in Richard Wentworth being discovered on the scene of action. He smiled at the high lifting of his heart. Gone was a curse from the world, a curse more deadly than any that had swept the cities of ancient Europe; the curse of that unholy alliance, politics and crime....

His thoughts broke off as a flash of movement caught his eye. He had a glimpse of a face, the forehead pocked by a false bullet-hole. His gun swung up, belching a challenge of death as he pivoted. Too late. Even as his finger tightened on the trigger, the man had whirled left behind the protection of thick walls. He had fled into the men's room.

With a furious shout, Wentworth sprang forward. In some inconceivable way, the Fiddler had escaped! Even in that fleeting glimpse, he had recognized the disguise that the other had assumed—that of Dodson Larrimore—and on the forehead, the false bullet hole which marked the means of his intended death.

He was still twenty feet from the doorway through which the Fiddler had dodged when the whine of bullets past his head, the hammer of a machine gun behind him, heralded an attack.

Wentworth threw himself down violently to the floor, only saving his skull from deadly impact with the floor by throwing his arm up in the way. With the impetus of his fall he rolled into the protection of rows of heavy seats, and caught a glimpse, through lowered eyelids, of a machine gunner. The gangster hurried forward, muzzle still pointed at his victim. Wentworth's guns had flown from his hands with the violence of his fall and he lay helpless, awaiting the killer—helpless while the Death Fiddler was escaping.

Wentworth could see the gangster with a terrible clarity now, could even see the vertical crease between his eyes as he prepared to kill; saw the tightening of his trigger finger....

A shot came from at least fifty feet away.

Even while he was still dazedly watching the machine gunner's arms sag with the weapon, his knees turn to rubber under him—with a shout that was hoarse in his throat, Wentworth jumped to his feet.

He flung a swift glance about the waiting room, saw a man's back vanish through doors on the far side. The doors creaked back into place and Wentworth shook his head dazedly, dragged the back of one hand across his forehead. Good Lord, had the blow of his fall affected his senses? For a moment, a fleeting moment, he had thought he recognized that man disappearing through the door, the man whose timely shot had saved Wentworth's life. He had thought it was Jackson, who had served with Wentworth in France, who had turned down a commission to remain his sergeant, who had come to be his chauffeur when the war was finished. Wentworth should know his back, certainly. He had stared often enough at those broadly competent shoulders while Jackson drove. But Jackson was dead, had died confessing the Spider's sins. Wentworth longed mightily to pursue that man if for no other purpose than to thank him—but meanwhile the Death Fiddler might escape! The Fiddler first!

WENTWORTH STOOPED to snatch his guns, whirled toward the door through which the Fiddler had disappeared. This was no time to indulge in lunatic speculation. In that room the leader of all this terror might be making good his escape. Wentworth plunged toward the doors and, at the same instant, in from the concourse poured a stream of men in police blue. In the front rank, gripping a riot gun at his hip, was a policeman Wentworth knew—carrot-topped Cassidy who had been Kirkpatrick's outer guard. Evidently Flynn had put him back in harness.

The riot gun was on Wentworth and Cassidy's usually good-humored face was set in a grim mask. He was within an ace of pulling the trigger when Wentworth jerked his hands, guns and all, above his head. Cassidy stared into his face with belated recognition.

"God save ye, Mr. Wentworth," he gasped, "I nearly shot yez."

"The Fiddler's in there!" Wentworth pointed with his automatic toward the door of the wash room. "I saw him run in there."

There was a stir among the thick-pressed ranks and a lean, tall man, a fedora hat set with military preciseness upon his head, thrust through to the front. He had a tight, bony face, a pointed, strong nose, a straight-lipped mouth, a jutting crag of a chin.

"What is this?" he snapped.

Cassidy let his gun hang at his side and snapped to salute.

"If the Commissioner pleases, sir. This gentleman says the Death Fiddler is in the wash room."

Commissioner Flynn—Wentworth had recognized him the

instant he spotted the man's head above the blue-coated rank—looked Wentworth over frostily. Wentworth's hands hung at his sides now, the automatics pointed toward the floor. Flynn's eyes sought those, lifted to his face again.

"Your name?" Flynn demanded.

Wentworth's hard-pressed lips relaxed in a slight smile. Despite Kirkpatrick's hostility to this man, despite what appeared inefficient organizing, Wentworth could not but recognize the force and strength of this new Commissioner. Cassidy's manner was sufficiently military, and deferentially the police were waiting for a word from him.

"Richard Wentworth," Wentworth gave his name and nodded in brief greeting. "If I may suggest, Commissioner, I saw the Fiddler run into this room. That gangster back there threw down on me with the machine gun and I was delayed for a couple of minutes, but the Fiddler should still be in there."

Flynn nodded stiffly, jerked out an order to the police, and they went into the wash room, guns first, without any more hesitation than they would have executed squads left on parade. Wentworth strode beside the Commissioner and together they stared toward the swing half-door to the wash room proper.

"Come out!" Flynn's brisk voice was edged. "Come out, or we'll blow that room full of lead."

"Thank God, thank God," a thin voice wailed behind the partition. "Thank God you've come at last, Flynn." A man's tottering legs showed beneath the half-door and above it showed the eyes and roached black hair of the Mayor of New York City!

Wentworth's breath hissed sharply between his teeth. Once or twice before his suspicions had turned toward the Mayor, but he had discounted the man as lacking sufficient intelligence to carry out the Death Fiddler's crimes, or to plan them in the first place. But the Mayor's presence here was suspicious, extremely so.

"Is this the man you saw come in here?" Flynn asked Wentworth sharply.

Wentworth shook his head. "You know the Fiddler's trick of disguising himself to look like the man he intends to kill in his regular Thursday night murders?"

Flynn nodded jerkily. It was obvious that he wasted few words. His whole manner was swift; his gestures choppy, his long-legged stride almost violent in its impetuosity.

"Tonight," said Wentworth slowly, "the Death Fiddler was disguised as Dodson Larrimore."

THE MAYOR'S tight mouth dropped open in surprise and Flynn threw a sharp side glance at Wentworth. "Right," said Flynn. "Glimpsed him myself. Knew he looked familiar. Anyone enter there?" This last to the Mayor.

Purviss shook his head loosely and moved toward the policemen. Wentworth was frowning. Wasn't the man overdoing his surprise and fear just a little?

"Larrimore's in there," the Mayor stuttered.

Wentworth beat Flynn to the swing door, saw a man sprawled on the floor and stooped over him. He rolled the man over on his back, saw that it was really Larrimore and that he had been hit over the head. There was an automatic under his right hand.

Flynn looked up at Wentworth under brows which did not wrinkle. "Know Larrimore well?"

"Fairly," said Wentworth, copying the other's laconic speech. "Don't worry about identification. This is the man."

He wet a paper towel and sopped Larrimore's forehead. It was ten minutes before Larrimore recovered; then he jerked up, his arms flying to a defensive position. As soon as he realized who was about him, he sagged back to the floor and frowned, his eyes shutting with pain.

"What happened?" he asked thickly.

"You tell us," Flynn suggested sharply.

Larrimore opened his eyes, shading them with his palm, and stared up at the Commissioner. "Hello, Flynn," he said weakly. Then he nodded to Wentworth, after which he closed his eyes again and seemed to be thinking.

"I remember now," he said finally, his voice clearer. "Purviss and I were crouched in the outer room after we had run up from the Long Island platform. I had emptied my automatic and had no more bullets. We heard a heavy blast of firing, then some more in the waiting room just outside. Purviss went on back into the inner wash room and I waited, trying to decide just what to do. Then I heard another single shot just outside here and decided I'd get under cover, too. I walked toward the swing door. Then I heard footsteps behind me. Before I could turn, something hit me on the head and I fell toward the door. I got hit again as I went down."

Purviss, when questioned, told about the same story. He saw Larrimore falling through the door and dragged him inside out of sight for fear that someone might see the body and investigate. In his excitement, Purviss was quite candid about the reason for dragging Larrimore inside.

Wentworth looked about the anteroom. There was a side door at the other end which led out onto another main concourse, and two high windows which did the same. There had been minutes after the Fiddler had fled into this room when Wentworth had not been able to watch the door. What Larrimore and Purviss described was possible. He went back to where Larrimore stood shakily on his feet.

"Are you quite sure," he asked, "that you had not entered the wash room when you were hit?"

Flynn's flinty eyes held his face steadily, and Larrimore lifted his head with a tired smile.

"No, I can't say definitely," he said. "What I told you before is what I thought happened, but now that you ask me I'm not quite sure. Actually all I remember is turning away from the main door there and starting in to join Purviss."

A patrolman supported Larrimore as he walked on heavy feet toward the waiting room. He checked and turned slowly.

"Please don't say anything about this in the newspapers," he implored, "or mention that the Fiddler was dressed up like me. My wife would be worried to death."

Flynn jerked a nod and, when he had gone, looked toward Wentworth. "What's up?" he asked shortly.

Wentworth gestured toward the entry to the wash room and walked there with Flynn, then indicated the floor.

"Can you see," he asked, "where the body of a man was dragged along this floor?"

THE FLOOR was dirty, smeared with black tracks from wet shoes. Wentworth dragged his toe through the mess and it left a distinct trail. Flynn spat out an oath.

"Who's lying?" he demanded roughly.

Wentworth shrugged. "Larrimore told two stories, but Purviss confirmed that part about dragging him inside. Frankly, I don't know what to think. Larrimore was obviously confused. He might have been hit just as he went through the door, staggered two steps or more and fallen, just as a boxer may keep on going when he's out on his feet. That's especially true if Larrimore was moving swiftly. On the other hand...."

Flynn's hard blue eyes were steadily on his. "What?" he asked.

"On the other hand, Larrimore might have been hit over the head inside the door, by Purviss. As I pointed out, there is no evidence of anyone being dragged across the floor. I do not see how the Fiddler could have slugged Larrimore *inside the wash room* without being seen by Purviss... But if Purviss were in league with the Fiddler, it would have been a simple matter for him to strike down Larrimore as he came through the door."

Wentworth could see the stiffening of Flynn's ramrod back as he finished. But the Commissioner did not explode as he half expected. Instead, Flynn dropped his eyes again to the tell-tale floor.

"They say Kirkpatrick's holding his own," he said abruptly. "Makes me feel terrible, taking his job. He probably hates my guts." A wintry smile touched his lips as the army expression slipped out. "Hates me for kicking out Boice, flock of others. Had to, you know. They were loyal to Kirkpatrick. Naturally. Had to turn everything upside down. Show them who's boss. Old army trick." He drew a deep breath. "Kirkpatrick respected your judgment a lot. Know because I followed him closely. Newspapers, I mean. You think Purviss guilty?"

Wentworth felt a rising respect and liking for this stern, soldierly Commissioner. Flynn had actually offered an apology, an indirect one, it was true, for his retirement of Kirkpatrick's favorites. But his justification was sound—and his firm grip of the men was evident in the unquestioning obedience with which they had wheeled into the wash room in the face of what might have been instant death. So Wentworth hesitated before he spoke. The man had indicated he would give great weight to what he said.

"I don't know," he remarked finally. "Purviss had no chance to change his story. He might have said something he did not quite mean in his excitement. Maybe what he meant was that he caught Larrimore as he was falling and helped him a few faltering steps before he collapsed. Commissioner, the whole case is a great puzzle to me. Usually I have some very definite ideas about a man of the proportions of this fellow who calls himself the Death Fiddler. But I'm stumped this time. The only thing I can say with any certainty is that the Fiddler is either a politician or he has a life-and-death hold over someone who is a very powerful politician. And you see that covers a great deal of territory. I am explaining at such length because I would not want to lead you astray."

Flynn nodded. "Police work, deduction, is new to me. Can organize men. I'll snap the whole force up in short order. But deduction—" He shook his head. "Appreciate any help you can give." He offered his hand. Wentworth clasped it gladly. A firm, powerful grip Flynn had, and there was nothing old about his skin. It was elastic with youth.

When Wentworth returned to the Lancia a policeman bawled him out for parking in front of the station entrance and gave him a ticket.

CHAPTER 16
DEATH IN HERALD SQUARE

IT WAS afterward that Wentworth remembered to check on whether Raymond Allen had been in the Pennsylvania station at the time of the Death Fiddler's attack. When he did think of it he could only have private detectives ascertain whether Allen had an alibi.

Strangely, it was not the close involvement of Purviss with the raid, nor the attack on Larrimore, nor even the apparent friendliness of Flynn, which persisted in Wentworth's thoughts. It was his glimpse of the back of a man who had saved his life, the broad-shouldered one who had shot down the machine gunner in the instant he prepared to kill Wentworth.

Memory is a confusing thing. A few minutes after a man speaks, he probably will not be able to tell precisely what he said. The more intensively he thinks about the matter, the more muddled his memory tracks become. So it was with Wentworth. He could think only that the man's back had seemed to be Jackson's. But Jackson was dead. He had been buried with great military honor. It could not have been Jackson. And yet....

Wentworth's detectives could find no one who had seen Allen between the time he left some friends at a political club around four-thirty and his arrival at home three hours later. The detectives also discovered the reason for Purviss' and Larrimore's presence in the station. Purviss had dropped Larrimore by the station in his car on the way home and had, at Larrimore's invitation, dropped in on the Savarin restaurant and bar there for a cocktail. Larrimore was, of course, on his way home. He lived in Forest Hills where he was buying a house for his wife and two young children.

On the day after the tragedy the full casualties of the attack were finally computed. Six police, three ticket agents, and seventeen commuters had been killed. The criminal losses had been heaviest. Thirty-four had been slain, ten more taken to hospitals with serious wounds. Twenty-one had been shot down in the single phalanx in the center of which the Fiddler had attempted to make his escape.

The newspapers hailed the battle as a signal victory over the Death Fiddler and predicted that the city had heard the last of him. The news even checked slightly the steady average of holdups. But on Wednesday, two days after the battle, the crime wave rose to a new zenith and Wentworth went again to the Underworld to discover the reason. He went furtively, as Limpy Magee, and even dared to visit his shop, which the thin little girl with the shawl was patiently operating. She started violently when Wentworth, stealing up from the cellar, spoke gently in her ear. Then she whirled and flung her arms about his shoulders.

"Oh, Limpy," she sobbed, "they said you were dead! They said you were the Spider and that you were dead."

Wentworth patted her shaking shoulders, then detached himself gently. He went to a battered old desk, penned and pre-dated a paper giving her the shop, and handed it to her.

"I am the Spider," he told her gravely, "but I'm very far from dead. This shop is yours now. Sometimes I may come back here. Will you always have a room for me?"

"Oh, yes, yes!" The girl reached for him again, but Wentworth turned lightly away. He stole down into the basement, leaped halfway down and sprawled on the earthen floor with his gun in his hand.

"Stand just like that," he ordered fiercely.

THE FIGURE crouched against the light of the cellar door opening into the backyard, straightened slowly. "Okay, Limpy," he growled. "I just wanted to talk to you."

"Why in the hell didn't you say so?" snarled Limpy Magee. He crossed stiffly toward the figure, then hesitated. "Bill Horace!" he grunted.

"Yeah, me," the policeman admitted. "Listen, mug, are you the Spider?"

Wentworth laughed softly, the mocking flat laughter men knew and feared everywhere as heralding that dread avenger of the night. Gone, abruptly, were the rough manners of Limpy Magee. But he held his gun steadily on the policeman.

"Why yes, William," he agreed gently. "I am the Spider. But

"If any man moves, the Death Fiddler dies—The Spider swears it!"

don't get any ideas into your head that you're going to collect the reward."

Horace laughed harshly. "Not me," he said. "I knew there was something funny about you from the first. But you done me some good turns. Just the same, if I ever bump into you when I'm on duty, I'm going to run you in."

"Certainly, William."

"Don't call me William," the policeman said crossly. "Listen, I've found out why crooks are getting all set up again. Half of the Fiddler's mob is still going strong. Even losing the loot of the Penn Station and the Metropolitan ain't stopped them. They're planning some big job tomorrow. I can't find out what."

"Ah," said Wentworth softly. "Where can I call you, Willie—pardon me, Bill—if I should want to reach you?"

The policeman gave his false name and the number of a cheap hotel where he was staying. "Listen, Spider," he said slowly, "you seen Tony lately? Tony Musette, the girl who was with my brother at the saloon that night?"

"I hear of her," Wentworth said. "She is well. I hear that she and Jerry are still trying to get poor old Limpy Magee for killing you."

"Hell, you can't blame them."

"I don't, Bill," Wentworth told him. "Now, kindly go upstairs into the shop. I want to hear you lock the door up there."

"I ain't out for you, Spider."

"Of course not," Wentworth agreed. "Go upstairs."

His retreat from the Underworld being thus uneventful, Wentworth spent the evening with Nita trying desperately to figure out what the Fiddler's next move would be. Flynn accepted the information already gleaned with monosyllabic thanks. He would have men ready at all stations on the next day for an emergency, he said. Wentworth believed that the plans would be thorough. An army man would know how to organize such things. Thoughtfully, he called Larrimore.

"Can you tell me Purviss' movements for tomorrow?" he asked.

Larrimore said: "I'm sorry he's not in. I'll have him call you later." By that, Wentworth understood that Larrimore was not in a position for talking. Since the wounding of Kirkpatrick, Larrimore had repeatedly called to give him information which might be valuable in his fight against the Death Fiddler, or in helping Kirkpatrick's campaign.

Kirkpatrick's foes were hammering at the fact that he had resigned from office in the midst of one of the worst crime waves in history and they had broadcast one of those sly questions which cannot be branded libel.

"We ask Kirkpatrick," ran the question, "if it is not a fact that the Mayor asked him to resign because of his inefficiency in combating the rising tide of crime?"

Purviss professed himself unable to find a copy of the letter he had sent to Kirkpatrick and no one had been able to locate the original among Kirkpatrick's papers. It was a cowardly attack against a man who could not answer back and among some people it stirred resentment. Others, influenced by the opposition claims that Kirkpatrick really was not badly wounded but was seeking to avoid answering their challenges, had turned against Kirkpatrick.

The hospital reported impersonally that "Mr. Kirkpatrick had a slightly more restful night. He is holding his own."

Even if Kirkpatrick recovered, he would be too weak to campaign. That was certain. Only one thing could save the election for him, or clear his name of the mud that had been thrown upon it by political foes. That would be for him somehow to smash the Death Fiddler.

Wentworth laughed bitterly at the thought. How could Kirkpatrick, battling for his very life in the hospital, conquer the Fiddler? If Wentworth could learn the man's plans and defeat them, then give the credit to Kirkpatrick… But that would be immediately suspect. No, there must be some other way.

LARRIMORE'S CALL elicited nothing spectacular for the following day, Thursday. Purviss would be in his office practically all day. He had refused all appointments because he had a conference with bankers for the afternoon over a loan to the city. Larrimore laughed a little nervously when Wentworth asked him what protection he himself was planning for the following night.

"It doesn't seem to make much difference what form of protection a man has," he said. "The Fiddler managed to get the Governor despite nearly a hundred guards. What chance have I got?"

It was two o'clock the following afternoon, Thursday, when Larrimore called him excitedly. "I don't know what this means," he said rapidly, "but Purviss has just sent me on the most nonsensical errand I ever heard of."

Wentworth frowned, rubbed his palm across his forehead. He had been working furiously to find an answer to the Fiddler's return of confidence, and he had failed. "What is it?" he asked wearily.

"He just ordered me to go to Macy's to get him some personal stationery," Larrimore replied. "The funny part of it is that he's got all the personal stationery he needs. And, anyway, he has a half dozen lesser men to run errands for him. Yet he sends me…" Larrimore hesitated. "I confess I'm uneasy."

All Wentworth's suspicions of Purviss arose anew. As Larrimore said, it was a strange thing the Mayor had ordered. Was there a reason behind it? Wentworth knew that the Death Fiddler planned a new outrage today—and he had been unable to learn where the man planned to strike, or when.

"Did Purviss tell you any special time to get there?" Wentworth asked slowly.

"That's another strange thing," Larrimore went on, growing more and more worried. "He said that the woman he wanted me to see went out at two-thirty for lunch and I absolutely had to get there by that time."

Wentworth's fist hit the telephone stand a blow that made the receiver jar against his ear. "Don't go," he told Larrimore quickly. "Without a doubt, the Fiddler is planning to rob Macy's store today!"

He hung up, signaled excitedly for the operator. His remark to Larrimore had been sheer guesswork, but the more he thought of it the more certain he was that his surmise was correct. Macy's receipts for the day undoubtedly topped that of any other store in town. What was it their advertisements said—four sales every second? The total would be enormous, somewhere up in the hundreds of thousands. He was suddenly certain Macy's was the object of the attack.

Why then had Purviss directed Larrimore to go to the store? But that, too, was rather obvious. Suspicion already had pointed partly to Larrimore because of the affair in Penn Station, though there it had touched the Mayor also. If Larrimore were at Macy's at the time that the robbery was staged and was found there, if he presented the nonsensical excuse that he had just given Wentworth over the phone and then Purviss denied having sent Larrimore to the store, the secretary would certainly be in bad spot.

In the same instant that the explanation of Purviss' strange order had struck Wentworth, another thought had occurred. He wanted some way of thwarting the Fiddler and throwing the credit to Kirkpatrick. Well, he knew the Fiddler's plans now, and abruptly he realized how he could throw the credit to Kirkpatrick.

Bill Horace undoubtedly still carried the handwritten order from Kirkpatrick directing him to let the story of his deal remain uncontradicted and to investigate the Fiddler. If, then, Bill Horace should phone in the tip on what was to occur, the credit would go to Kirkpatrick for having assigned an astute man to the case and, at the same time, having seized on a man reported dead to do the work....

THE CALL went through and a nasal voice asked roughly what was wanted. Wentworth asked for Horace under the assumed name he used and waited through interminable minutes.

"Yeah?" Bill Horace's voice was as laconic and rough as the first that had answered.

"Bill," Wentworth said swiftly. "this is Limpy Magee. I found out what the Fiddler is goin' to do this p.m. Yeah, at two-thirty he's going to rob Macy's. Yeah. Now listen Bill, you call up Flynn and don't talk to nobody else. Tell him you learned all about it from a friend you've got who's in on the Fiddler's gang."

Horace's voice was heavy. "Sure, I'll tell him I got it from my brother. Why in the hell didn't you tell me Jerry was nuts about the Fiddler? Cheez, if I'd stayed home I might of saved the kid."

"You didn't stand a chance," Wentworth snapped at him. "He's killed two men, killed them before you ever had that little run-in with Limpy Magee at Collins' place. I could cite you facts. But don't delay, Bill. It's ten after two now and the Fiddler is going to hit at two-thirty. Tell Flynn that Kirkpatrick gave you that special assignment, then hand the paper over to him when you go in and if he doesn't boost you to a detective, I miss my guess a long way. Hurry, Bill. Man, a thousand lives depend on you!"

Wentworth hung up and sat tensely by his telephone. A thousand lives might not be much of an exaggeration. If the robbers cut loose with machine guns in the crowded aisles of the big department store on Herald Square, there would be plenty of bloodshed. And the evil would not end there. A successful looting of Macy's would stir the Underworld to rabid frenzy again. It would loot and kill for the sheer joy of crime.

Five minutes by his watch, Wentworth waited, until he was sure Bill Horace had had time to put his call through. Then he, too, phoned Commissioner Flynn. He got Police Headquarters, but was told Flynn was too busy to talk.

"This is Wentworth," he rasped imperatively. "If you want to take the responsibility for a thousand murders just keep me from talking to Flynn."

In a moment Flynn barked his name into the phone.

"The Fiddler is going to raid Macy's at two-thirty," Wentworth rushed his words.

Flynn interrupted, demanding to know where he had got the information, jerking out that a policeman who had been reported dead had phoned in the same thing not two minutes before. Wentworth told what he knew from Larrimore and now and then Flynn interrupted to bark orders at what apparently was a chain of orderlies darting in and out of his office.

"The Fiddler has been planning something spectacular," Wentworth concluded his brief marshaling of the facts. "What could he do more spectacular than looting the city's largest store?"

"Sounds crazy," Flynn said sharply, "but from two sources, this way, it must be so. Police are covering."

"Good," Wentworth snapped. "See you there."

He slammed down the phone and sprang from his chair. It was two-twenty, ten minutes before the Death Fiddler was to strike. He ran for the door, patting his under-shoulder holsters as a matter of habit to be sure he had his guns.

"Jenkyns," he called, "call Miss Nita. At Macy's—you know how. Tell her to get out quickly, that in ten minutes the Death Fiddler will raid the store."

Wentworth knew that he was speaking foolishness even as he requested Jenkyns to act. It was well that Nita should be warned in advance, but she would no more leave the scene of action than Wentworth would stay away himself.

A TAXI spun Wentworth swiftly down and across town. At the Seventh Avenue entrance of Macy's he alighted with two minutes to spare. He caught an elevator to the third floor, knowing that one of the money receiving offices was on the fourth. As he wove a rapid way through crowds that packed the store, there was a leaping joy in his heart because he had once more ferreted out the Death Fiddler's plot.

Yet his lips were drawn tight and straight with apprehension. In this crowd, the police would fear to shoot, but no such consideration would deter the criminals. Wentworth began to realize that the plan to rob the store was not as mad as it had first seemed. So far as escaping was concerned, the very crowds would facilitate it.

Flight outside might be a different matter. South of Times Square, no street carried half so much traffic as Thirty-fourth, just outside Macy's front door. To the west on Seventh Avenue, traffic would be impossibly congested, too, since Macy's was just at the edge of the Pennsylvania Station district as well as the heavy trucking of the garment district, with Times Square itself only a short distance northward.

On the east was the junction of Broadway and Sixth Avenue, the two triangles of Herald Square and Greeley Square. Here again, with street car lines on both avenues, and on Thirty-fourth as well, with the pillars of the elevated further complicating traffic, escape seemed cut off. Thirty-fifth would be blocked with trucks and was narrow at best.

Wentworth nodded as he recounted these things in mind. Undoubtedly Flynn would plan to stop the bandits as they attempted to flee the store. He would not invade the building itself where stray bullets might kill more than had died in the Pennsylvania Station battle. Now that he recalled the scraps of Flynn's orders heard over the phone, he was convinced that this was the Commissioner's plan.

Wentworth threading his way along the third floor, was still fifty feet away from the down escalators when he saw the first indication of the raid. He had planned to cover those moving steps, block them against possible escape, hoping that Flynn was planning some similar guard on stairs and elevators. Even if Flynn had not yet had time to take such precautions, Wentworth hoped to delay the escape until police could make sure of capture by posting large forces of reserves about the store. Flynn would be at his best in such an effort.

A sharp curse rasped in Wentworth's throat and he tried to worm his way more rapidly through the thickening throng of shoppers. The aisle ahead was completely blocked by a four-deep crowd about a counter where a sign read *"$2.98 silks $1.49 a* *yard.*"Beyond, against the left hand wall, was the money reception office, a wooden partition with bronze-caged windows at regular intervals.

Abruptly the door at the end of the office opened and three men came out fast. The second carried two large leather bags, plumply stuffed, and the other two walked close on his flanks, heads down, hands thrust deep into bulging pockets. A glance assured Wentworth that these, the money carrier and two guards, were some of the men he had come to block.

He estimated distances rapidly. He was fifty feet from the end of the downward escalator, pocketed behind a thick crowd of milling women shoppers. The three men had less than twenty-five feet to go and there was no crowd to block their escape.

Wentworth's hands itched for his automatics, but they, too, would be futile. If he charged violently through the crowd ahead, the three bandits would take alarm and blast their way free, mow down women and men indiscriminately with their desperate guns. He, himself, could not fire lest he wound someone....

FRANTICALLY WENTWORTH cast about for some means of blocking the escape. His eye lighted again on the silk bargain sign. With a grim smile he reached out and caught two women by the shoulders, hauled them out of the way, grabbed two more and wormed through the crowd to the counter. Shoppers jostled him and exclaimed indignantly. A slamming elbow caught him in the side and shortened his wind, but he reached the counter. With an easy spring, he was standing on its top amid the silks.

The three gangsters caught the sound of the disturbance

now. The man with the money quickened his pace. The other two stopped, shoulders tensing, hands half pulling from their pockets.

Wentworth caught up a bolt of silk, grabbed the loose end and heaved the bolt itself violently toward the gangsters. Its glittering length unwound across the store, above the heads of the startled women, toward the two armed guards. Their hands were clear of their pockets now, the ugly snouts of their automatics half raised.

At the same instant, Wentworth snatched his automatics from their holsters. Each blasted once. He had a clear shot over the heads of the frightened women, and the bullets flew true.

Both bandits reeled backward, guns dropping from their hands, startled pain on their faces. One struck a counter, spun about, and caught it with his hands as he went down. The counter tipped and spilled an avalanche of boxed silk stockings upon him.

The second gangster stared incredulously at Wentworth. The tag end of the bolt of silk still fluttered in the air, wavering downward to the floor. It had served its purpose well, bewildered the two gunmen while Wentworth got his guns into play. Then the man went down all at once, every joint collapsing simultaneously as he flopped forward on his face.

The man carrying the money twisted about. As he saw his two guards go down beneath the Spider's lead, a shrill scream tore from his lips and he sprang toward the escalator. Wentworth fired while he was still in mid-leap and the man went limp, arms and legs dangling, to come down in a heap on the topmost step of the moving stairway. The fat money bags landed soddenly on the floor.

Wentworth stood quietly for a moment, a hard smile on his lips. The body of the third dead gunman was moving downward on the escalator, being carried along with a majestic slowness which had in it a suggestion of the callous inevitability of fate. Women stood staring up at Wentworth, at the dead bandits, with open mouths, faces frozen in panic. It had all happened so quickly that fear had not yet released their lungs.

Then one woman screamed. She screamed again, took two faltering steps—and crumpled to the floor in a dead faint.

That one cry touched it off. With the suddenness of a shot, all the women were trampling madly back, anywhere from this calm madman with the two guns and those pitifully crumpled bodies.

Wentworth sprang to the floor and caught up the woman who had fainted. He laid her gently down upon the silk bargain counter, out of the way of the stampede, then loped to where the money bags lay. The one gunman's body was halfway to the floor below now, on the deliberately moving escalator....

WENTWORTH CAUGHT up the bags of money, ran to the office from which it had been stolen—and stopped there, staring down in horror. A girl lay upon the floor in an awkward position, which could mean only death. The back of her head had been crushed by a blow. Two men lay there also, bound hand and foot.

Wentworth quickly freed them, told them briefly what had

happened and what to expect. Then he hurried back to the escalator.

He ran rapidly down it. The moving steps were deserted now. Customers and clerks had fled from the second floor, fled from the proximity of the body that had ridden headfirst down the escalator and stubbornly refused to be entirely discarded. It lay at the bottom of the flight, half on, half off, the steps; each succeeding tread bending the toes of the man's shoes upward, then sliding on as the gentle thrust failed to stir the body.

Wentworth pulled the man clear and ran with long strides along the second floor toward the head of the next escalator. This was where Nita was supposed to work with Tony Musette. But he saw nothing of the girls. Perhaps, after all, Nita had obeyed his warning and left the store. Yet he doubted that.

He flung a swift glance about him, looked at the elevator bank across the floor. With a leaping exultation he saw that the indicators, showing on which floor the cars were stationed, were not moving. That meant that all the elevators had been halted....

With a tight smile, Wentworth realized also that it meant the bandits now would have to use either escalators or ordinary stairs—with the odds in favor of the escalators. He opened the clips of his automatics and replaced the cartridges he had fired. Quickly reconnoitering his position, he saw that he was exposed from the doorway giving on the stairs, and from the back escalators. If he moved that counter on his right, it would give him protection from the rear.

He stepped toward the counter—and heard a man's frightened shout from above. His eyes narrowed, his lips stirred in a hard smile. Had the bandits discovered their dead? It was probable. He watched the moving railing of the escalator above him and saw a man's hand grip it. As the stairs slid downward, more of the arm, then the shoulder, appeared, afterward the back of the man's head.

The man jerked about in swift alarm as if he sensed the Spider's watch. But the upward throw of his gun was too slow. Wentworth's shot drilled him through the head.

For a moment longer, the hand gripped the moving rail, then slid from sight. Wild curses rang out above. Wentworth circled widely to his left, got directly in front of the escalator. Two pairs of legs were visible at the top. He rested both automatics on a counter, sighted at the legs, and discharged both guns together. Two men's bodies came suddenly into view, one pitching on the escalator, the other scrabbling around at the top.

Up to this time, Wentworth's automatics had made the only gun sounds in the store. But now, suddenly, on the floor above a machine gun chattered. The man on the escalator tried an awkward shot and Wentworth drilled him also through the head. In another moment, three bodies were heaped sprawlingly at the foot of the escalator.

Wentworth thought quickly. He had held this means of descent without much trouble so far, but there was a persistent worry in the back of his mind. Considering the size of this operation, there was too little shooting. Either Flynn had not arrived on the scene, or the Fiddler's band had not left the store. Would they bunch and rush the lines?

A MACHINE gun sputtered on the enclosed stairway off

to Wentworth's left, apparently at the second floor level. Then the sound went on down, rattling noisily. Good Lord! That one machine gun loosed on the packed crowd below would slaughter scores, hundreds....

Wentworth darted for the down escalator. He crouched upon it so that his head just topped the wooden side, and peered toward the stairs exit. Four machine gunners were in line there and each had the muzzle of his weapon against the back of a woman. Before them was the whole massed crowd of the store, many of whom had descended from upper floors and jammed this one tight.

Behind the machine gunners were ten other men. And one, in the guise of Dodson Larrimore, with that bragging fake bullet wound between his eyes, was *the Death Fiddler himself!*

Wentworth's fingers trembled on the triggers of his automatics as he slid lower and lower on the escalator. But then a startled oath ripped from his throat. One of the women held captive below was Tony Musette, and another was... *was Nita!*

He had just time to discover that when the Fiddler's voice rang out in a stentorian order. "You by the door there, tell the police outside that unless we are allowed to go our way unmolested, not only these four girls, but everyone in front of these guns will be killed.

"Tell them, furthermore, that we have another recourse which should keep the police here until we are well on our way. There are a dozen bombs planted in this building, enough to bring the entire structure crashing down upon your heads. We are willing to wait in here until those bombs go off. It would be no more fatal to us than going out the door there. But if we are allowed to go free, we will phone back the location of the switch that controls the bombs in time to prevent the destruction of the building and all those in it."

Wentworth had reached the bottom of the escalator by the time the man had finished his speech. He heard people near the door shout the message to the police outside.

"Tell the police they'd better hurry. The bombs will go off in twenty minutes," the Fiddler shouted.

There was something wrong about all this, Wentworth told himself fiercely. If the Fiddler had one good feature it was the fact that he would not tolerate any objectionable behavior toward women. Yet this time their successful escape hinged exclusively on the threatened destruction of women.

Was it possible that all the man's previous chivalry had been a sham? Wentworth did not believe it. Why, the Fiddler had twice killed his own men simply to preserve that tradition!

Still puzzling over the discrepancy as he slipped through the crowd to the up-bound escalator and allowed it to carry him higher, Wentworth's every muscle was tense, while madness ran through his brain. How in the name of heaven was he to defeat the Death Fiddler? Those bombs would destroy the building and all within it even if the Spider managed to free the hostages of his machine guns.

And even that much seemed an impossible task. There were four men with machine guns, another with a revolver. One person could not possibly account for all five before the murderous hail of lead was turned lose. To be sure, he could save Nita by a single well-placed shot, but her release alone would not serve. There must, *must* be a way!

AS THE escalator carried him from sight, Wentworth cast a last frantic glance about. And suddenly hope burgeoned within him. He would have to work fast. All his chances depended on speed, on the Fiddler remaining where he was for a few minutes longer. A few minutes… Good Lord! Within twenty minutes, the building would come tumbling down upon all the thousands packed into that first floor and held there by guns!

Wentworth darted first to the men's clothing department, against the east wall of the building. From its cases, he whipped a black felt hat and a black Inverness cape. A black scarf furnished a mask when he had slashed eyeholes with his knife. Then he raced back across the floor and down a short flight of stairs to the balcony just above the Death Fiddler's head.

As he ran he swiftly looped a length of the powerful silk cord which he always carried with him, the silk cord that was less than the diameter of a lead pencil but which had a tensile strength of seven hundred pounds. Reaching the balcony, he crept to the railing, behind a silk shawl draped over the edge.

"Time is flying," the Death Fiddler boomed, just below him. "It is only fifteen minutes before the bombs explode."

Wentworth had his loop ready. He straightened, leaned over the railing, and made his cast. His appearance had scarcely registered on the assembled crowd, the murmur of fright and surprise had only begun to rise from their throats, when the silken loop settled about the neck of the Fiddler.

With a jerk, Wentworth drew the loop tight. He hauled

upward until the Fiddler could barely touch his toes to the counter below. Dexterously he drew the cord about a pillar, fastened its end to the leg of a heavy table, then balanced the table on the railing.

"If any man moves," Wentworth shouted, "the Death Fiddler dies. *The Spider swears it!*"

Gangsters and machine gunners stared upward with twisted necks. "Stand still," Wentworth warned them. "If you move, I'll drop the table. The line is around this pillar and the yank of the table will break the Fiddler's neck. Shoot me and the same thing happens. At present, your leader, though a bit uncomfortable, can still survive." He sent his mocking flat, laughter over the assembled crowd.

It was deadlock, and a deadlock which only the Spider could break. The gangsters held their guns on the crowd, but if they shot anyone, or attempted to shoot the Spider—even if they succeeded in killing him!—their leader died and that meant an end of them. They knew they could never get out without him.

Wentworth had hit upon the one possible way out of the situation and with his usual swift facility had seized upon it.

"Will you young ladies down there kindly relieve those gentlemen of the machine guns?" Wentworth asked, mockingly. "Ah, ah!" he warned one of the men who resisted, "Be careful or I'll break your dear Fiddler's neck!"

Nita held a machine gun in competent hands now, trained on the men who had held her prisoner.

"Now then," said Wentworth, "we'll wait for the bombs to go off. You ladies out there can make your way quietly out of the doors. These men lied about the amount of time remaining before the bombs went off. You have plenty of time, but get moving at once."

The Spider peered benevolently down upon the crowd and a slow movement toward the door started. Wentworth glanced at his watch nervously. He had lied about extra time, of course, but he had done it to prevent the panic that the truth might have caused. Once they were moving in orderly fashion toward the door, it would be easy to speed them up without danger. Wentworth leaned forward, with his elbows on the railing.

"I wonder if any of you gentlemen would be kind enough to tell us where the switch to the bomb is?" he asked gently.

"Hands up!" a man's voice spoke behind him. "Hands up, Spider! And keep them up."

Wentworth straightened with a cold fear prodding at his heart—fear for those hundreds, those thousands packed helplessly below him, awaiting death. He knew that voice and he knew what it portended.

"Get that table down off the railing," the voice went on. Jerry Horace's voice.

The Spider had made a clever play, had had the victory virtually in his hands. And now, through this man, he might lose it all; sacrifice the lives of all these men and women.

What chance had he, with Jerry Horace behind him with a gun? What chance to save those thousands who could not possibly escape from the building before the bombs went off? There was an awful tension in all his muscles, a rigidity in his neck. Despairing rage narrowed his eyes. He would not give up. He *could* not....

"I can't put up my hands, Jerry." Nothing of that tension nor rage showed in his voice. "I can't put my hands up because, if I do, the Fiddler will die!"

CHAPTER 17
SURRENDER

JERRY HORACE'S voice sounded from closer behind Wentworth; a gun prodded into his ribs.

"Get that table down off the railing," Jerry ordered tightly.

The Spider's face grew rock hard under the black mask that covered it. Many times now he had been on the point of victory over the Death Fiddler, and each time some one thing had prevented his triumph. The breath came quickly between his teeth, the slow, hard pounding of his heart seemed to echo throughout his entire body. Even if it meant his death, the death of all those hundreds grouped tensely below, the Fiddler should die this time. And his death would be a public execution! He would be hanged by the neck until dead, dead, dead....

"All right, Jerry," Wentworth said harshly. "I'll take the table off the railing."

He stepped back, deliberately shoved the heavy table. But he shoved it forward, so that with a lurch and a shriek of metal on wood it plunged downward toward the counters below.

Wentworth heard a rising, murmurous gasp from the waiting hundreds, heard the rope rasp about the pillar as the plunging table jerked it tight. Then the table crashed against the floor below, the rope whipped taut, and something black and limp jerked into view. The snap of the line had jerked the Death Fiddler clear of the counter and thrown him violently into the air. Only an instant was the body visible, then it plunged downward again. The line once more went taut and there was a dull snap that made Wentworth's lips skin back from his teeth. That sound was the breaking of the Death Fiddler's neck!

A great exultant joy surged over him. Come what might now, the Fiddler was dead. His gangs no longer would spread death and horror.... As the heat of jubilation swept over him, he pivoted on his heel.

Jerry Horace was staring with wide eyes, and dead white face. He was actually paralyzed, as if with both surprise and pain, at what he had seen.

No more than two seconds had passed since Wentworth had said harshly, "All right!" Yet in those two seconds, the Fiddler had died. And now....

Whirling, Wentworth's left hand slapped aside the leveled gun, his right closed about Jerry's throat. Thumb and fingers gouged home. For a moment the two stood motionless like that, then, with a sharp wrench, the Spider yanked the gun away and thrust Jerry backward three staggering paces. The Spider's flat laughter rippled from his lips. His chest was pumping with the joy of his laughter. He felt strong, invincible. The Fiddler was dead! The Spider had killed him!

"Now, Jerry," Wentworth snapped, "unless you want Tony

to be mashed to pieces when this building caves in, you'd better show me where that bomb switch is."

He laughed again. Nothing could beat him now. The bombs? Of course Jerry would talk.

"Run, Tony! Run!" Jerry shouted.

Wentworth shook his head. "She's standing by the girl she works with, Jerry, and by you. She wouldn't run and leave you to die. Are you going to let *her* die?" Wentworth's voice was taunting; the blind feeling of victory was still strong within him. Behind him, dangling at the end of a slender silken cord, the body of the Death Fiddler swung above the heads of his men. Nita held a machine gun on the others.

He laughed again. "Suppose that iron beam up there came down on Tony, Jerry? The result wouldn't be pretty, would it, Jerry? Rather ruin the shape of that lovely body...."

"Don't, for God's sake," Jerry gasped. "I'll show you the switch. I'll show you...."

HE TOTTERED away from the counter to which he had been hurled, looped about, started for the steps upward. Wentworth reached him in a long stride, jammed the gun against his ribs.

"We've got two minutes," he said in a flat, dry voice. His mouth felt arid. In the midst of his victory, was death to come, death from the bombs? *"Hurry, damn you!"*

Jerry went up the steps in leaping strides, wove among the counters toward the elevator shaft. His hip caught a counter and it knocked him aside, he tripped over a high stool and spilled down on his face, hands thrown out above his head... He scrambled up, lungs pumping, face agonized.

Wentworth shook him violently by the arm. "Quick, man! The switch!"

Jerry lifted a limp hand toward the shaft wall. "Box," he gasped. "Black box!"

With a hoarse shout, Wentworth sprang toward the box. A clock on the wall nearby showed there was only thirty seconds, thirty seconds to death... He wrenched open the box, snatched the switch clear.

A swift step behind him pulled him about and he dodged aside. There was no time even to draw breath, no time to exult that the bomb switch had been wrenched clear, that the thousands below were safe.

Jerry had played him a trick in that stumbling fall, a trick to make him leap ahead. The gang youth was on his feet now and in his hand he grasped the stool over which he had fallen. Even as Wentworth whirled about, the stool was swung heavily.

Wentworth flung up his arm. Barely diverting the blow, the down swing still caught him with sufficient force to numb his left arm and drive him to his knees.

With a hoarse shout, Jerry whirled the thing aloft, to strike again. Wentworth dived at his legs. He felt knees gouge into his shoulders, heard a thud as Jerry's head struck the wall. Then Wentworth was reeling to his feet and staring down at his unconscious assailant.

He shook his head sharply, drew up his left arm twice, clenching the fist with a grimace for the pain it caused, then ran swiftly toward the escalators.

As he ran, guns began to speak below—muffled at first, but growing louder as he neared the steps. He went down them in great bounding strides, an automatic in each hand. His keen eyes took in the scene below in a single sweeping glance.

Police were battling their way in through the doors. The packed hordes of shoppers were fighting their way outward, screaming, struck at last with panic. The rescue force was jammed inextricably. Before they could enter....

Wentworth swung toward the balcony. Sharp joy struck through him again at sight of the dangling figure of the Death Fiddler, swaying with a slow macabre rhythm above the heads of his fighting cohorts.

But his joy was short-lived. His swift eyes sought—and failed—to find Nita. His ready guns delayed....

Then he saw her, saw her supine upon the floor while above, legs straddled protectingly over her body, stood a broad-shoul-dered man who fought with the strength of the devil himself.

Even as Wentworth caught sight of him, the broad-shoul-dered fellow struck out savagely with a fist, slammed a gangster to the floor, and scooped up the machine gun the other had held. Wentworth saw a man throw down on him and his own automatic spoke with the instinctive swift speed of which only the Spider's was capable. The gangster's body jerked; he swayed, bent chin to chest, then pitched forward like that.

BESIDE NITA, the man with the machine gun crouched now and the gun began to chatter, sweeping from side to side.

Wentworth fired carefully from where he stood. He sprang from the escalator to its wooden side and, halting there, fired carefully, one shot at a time, picking out a gangster head here, a threatening gun hand there…. But his thoughts were not upon his guns. His thoughts were with that broad-shouldered one who crouched over Nita's body and fought like an inspired fiend.

Those shoulders identified the man as the one who had saved Wentworth's life in the raid on Pennsylvania Station. There could be no doubt about that. And in glimpsing those shoulders again and yet again as he swept his eyes over the press below seeking a new target, he felt a warm, thrilling certainty grow within him. Now, each time he squeezed the trigger, he said: "Jackson." He punctuated every shot with that word, either aloud or in his mind.

It couldn't be Jackson. It *couldn't* be. Jackson was dead, had died confessing the sins of the Spider. It was impossible….

Wentworth's automatic swerved upon a leaping figure which sprang toward the broad-shouldered one, but he held his fire just in time. It was Ram Singh. Nita, too, was alert now. Thrusting up on one arm, she was wielding a revolver. The three were a rallying point against the gangsters. Ram Singh had a long knife in each hand. He stood squarely behind the man with the machine gun, whose broad shoulders were hidden from Wentworth then….

The Spider's mind was whirling. Ram Singh and the other were fighting side by side as Jackson and Ram Singh had fought so many times. From behind the press of the battle, a gangster drew a bead on the machine gunner, and Ram Singh's swift knife became a flitting gleam of steel. It caught the gangster in the throat and the man went down in a sea of fighting killers. Wentworth saw that the machine gunner on his knees threw back his head and laughed.

Impossible to hear the sound of the laughter in the bedlam below. Impossible to hear anything except the screams of the wounded and dying, the panic yelp of fleeing women, the heavy pound of gunfire. Impossible, and yet Wentworth was sure he heard that laughter—such vaunting, battle-glorying laughter as only one man had ever uttered before…. A lump caught in his throat as a wild, fantastic hope made his heart leap. He sprang to the steps, started downward…. A stool hurled from the head of the steps caught him at the base of the neck. Only the fact that he was moving in the same direction prevented fatal injury. Even as it was, he went down violently upon the escalator, merely falling by impulse so that he landed on his shoulders instead of his head.

Down the moving steps, a man came running, his lips writhing in hate. It was Jerry Horace. He came down the steps in great vaulting strides, caught up the stool he had hurled and raised it slowly, tensely above his head. If that blow fell, the Spider would never stir again, never again carry the battle to the enemies of mankind. Jerry paused a moment with the stool poised, gloating with a small hating smile over his conquest.

"You killed Bill," his voice was shrill. "I swore I'd kill you for it."

BUT NITA had caught sight of the caped figure plunging down the steps, had seen that cowardly blow from behind. Frantic, she leveled her revolver and pulled the trigger. The hammer snapped futilely upon an empty chamber. She caught desperately at Ram Singh's leg. Her shout was barely audible above the sound of conflict, but her rigidly pointing revolver showed Ram Singh where danger lay....

He did not wait to turn. Twisted only from the hips, he whipped his knife forward like the missile of a catapult, in a throw fully seventy-five feet. The slim blade whistled with the speed of its passage, just as the stool was started downward....

Jerry stood rigidly, staring with wide, frightened eyes at the knife that had pierced his left arm through and through. His blow never fell upon the Spider. The stool dropped from his hands and he turned and fled wildly into the thick of the crowd.

Even while Ram Singh raced toward him, Wentworth staggered heavily to his feet, holding his head between squeezing palms. He thought nothing of the blow, nothing of the pain in his brain. The hammer of guns was suddenly stilled and he reeled toward where Nita came slowly, limping on the arm of the man who had defended her with a machine gun. Behind them lay the thick-piled rows of dead and over them swayed the body of the Death Fiddler, dancing on air at the end of that lethal Spider web.

Then Wentworth saw the face of the man beside Nita. He stopped and a great breath rushed into his lungs. He shook his aching head, dragged an incredulous hand across his eyes and stared again. He groped for a support, staggered back two full paces until his hips hit a counter. Then he leaned there, panting. A great cry burst from him.

"Jackson!" he cried. "Jackson!"

The man with the wide shoulders grinned almost sheepishly, his broad-jawed face flushed. Then he stiffened and saluted in perfect army style.

"If the Major pleases," he said formally, "Sergeant Jackson reports back for duty."

Wentworth pushed himself away from the counter only by an enormous physical effort. His feet dragged as he swayed forward. He whispered, "But damn it, man, I saw you die!"

The whisper, however, was held back by the lump in his throat. This was the man he had mourned for dead. This was the man he had seen yield up his life to save the Spider. And Jackson was alive and standing before him! Wentworth shook his head again. Then a quirky smile touched his lips.

"Damn it, Sergeant," he said grimly. "Damn it. You've been A.W.O.L. Your excuses had better be good!"

For a moment longer, the two men stood like that. Then Wentworth sprang forward and threw his arms about Jackson's broad shoulders. His hands patted the sturdy back, he leaned back and gripped Jackson by his arms. Their smiles were so wide their jaws hurt.

Nita said: "Dick, here comes Commissioner Flynn."

For a moment, the idea didn't penetrate, then Ram Singh whipped the damning Spider cape and hat from Wentworth and tossed them behind a counter. Wentworth stepped back, still grinning.

"Damn your soul, Jack, I believe I'm glad to see you," he said. "We'll talk tonight. There's work now."

THEIR SMILES left them. They were once more man and

master. Wentworth swung about and saw the high, bobbing head of Flynn come toward him. Jackson fell back and Wentworth called a greeting.

"The Spider beat us to it," Wentworth said. He nodded up at the swinging body.

"Heard about it," Flynn snapped. "Cut him down," he barked as one of his men rushed up.

The policeman raced up the steps to the balcony, cut the silken cord, lowered the body until it lay flat upon one of the counters. Both Flynn and Wentworth crossed to the spot. Wentworth still felt dazed. Jackson's resurrection was incredible, but he could not doubt its reality. Jackson had been dead and now....

Wentworth forced his attention to focus upon the man who lay flat on his back upon the counter. The Death Fiddler. There was no evidence of strangulation upon the face. The color was natural. Wentworth frowned, reached out and yanked at Fiddler's hair. It came loose—and with it came a mask, a steel mask that covered the entire face.

Wentworth gasped. Flynn said: "So, Danny Dawson was the Death Fiddler!"

Wentworth stared down at the dead face of the little crook, and slowly a bitter smile touched his lips. He shook his head sadly, disappointedly. "No," he said, "Danny Dawson wasn't the Fiddler." He had seen Dawson and the Fiddler side by side, many times! Danny was not the Fiddler. And that meant....

The world spun dizzily for Wentworth. That meant that the Fiddler had escaped! That he had never come to Macy's, had merely sent an underling to act in his place. The Death Fiddler was still at large! Humanity was still threatened by his diabolical plans, his wholesale murders!

CHAPTER 18
THE DEATH FIDDLER
IN PERSON

THE KNOWLEDGE that the murderous Fiddler was still at large, still able to muster his thieving, slaying cohorts, had overshadowed Wentworth's joy even in Jackson's return. He had been unable to convince Flynn that Danny Dawson was not the Death Fiddler. It had been, naturally, impossible to give evidence of seeing the two side by side. The information would be tantamount to confessing that he was the Spider. And short of that, there had been only the meager proof that the Fiddler was always chivalrous toward women.

Wentworth felt an immense weariness. He had thought the battle won, and now it was to begin all over again. Even the one clue he had had, Danny's connection with the Fiddler, was wiped out....

Resolutely, Wentworth thrust despair from him, turned toward where Ram Singh and Jackson stood respectfully in the doorway. Jackson was once more in his chauffeur's uniform, Ram Singh looked resplendent in the white he loved to wear about the house: long tunic, loose trousers, spotless turban across his dark, fine brows... There was still amazement in Wentworth's eyes as he regarded Jackson.

"It won't do, Jackson," he said gravely. "That dying confession of yours... The police will be on your neck if you come back."

"I'm my twin brother," Jackson said jauntily. "Mr. Kirkpatrick won't be Commissioner any more. We don't need to worry about that."

Wentworth laughed, his joy at Jackson's return thrusting back the clouds of despair.

"Ram Singh, brave warrior," he said, "there is no reward I could give which would show you my appreciation. Or wait... There is a sword you fancy..." Ram Singh's eyes grew brilliant. He swept a low *salaam*, cupped hands to his forehead.

"It is an emperor's sword, *sahib!*"

Wentworth smiled slowly. "It is a brave man's sword and I give it gladly to a brave man." Well Wentworth knew that an offer of money to Ram Singh would be an insult. "But tell me, my brave one, how it happens that I gaze once more upon the living face of him I mourned as dead."

Ram Singh's face was grave. He waved a hand gracefully. "*Wah, sahib*, it was as nothing. Had *sahib* not been wounded, he would have done it himself. It was merely that through cowardice I was not wounded in the battle when you killed that vile one who called himself the Avenger...."

"Jackson," Wentworth interrupted. "I see that I'll have to ask you for details."

Jackson clapped Ram Singh on the back, stood with his strong blunt fingers gripping his shoulder. "The lad saw Mr. Kirkpatrick carry you out to the ambulance and saw a guard take his stand by me. And then he saw me move a finger or something of the sort. Knew I was alive. He went into an antechamber and emptied his gun, then when the guard came running to find out about the noise, Ram Singh knocked him for a loop."

Ram Singh's face was impassive. "The guard was a fool," he said quietly. "He stood there and waited for me to hit him."

Nita, on the davenport beside Wentworth, laughed delightedly. She joyed as much in these two strong men, in their devotion to Wentworth, as she did in Jackson's return. Their loyalty to her was equaled only by their devotion to Wentworth.

Wentworth said grimly, "If you two stall me off much longer on this story, I'm going to put you both on bread and water." JACKSON GRINNED and hurried on. "Ram Singh knew that police hadn't counted the dead at that time, so he got one of the dead gangsters and put the cape and Spider mask on him. Police hadn't seen the Spider's face. They didn't know me… So when Ram Singh ran out of the chamber with me on his shoulder, telling them I was only wounded, they gave him a hand to the taxi. They thought I was some friend of yours. Ram Singh took me to your doctor friend instead of to the hospital."

"Damn it, Ram Singh," Wentworth cut in. "Why didn't you tell me about all this? I might have helped. Jackson might have…" His throat closed. He swallowed hard and laughed a little uncertainly. "Get on with it," he ordered gruffly.

Jackson's eyes dropped to the floor. He hesitated a little before he went on. These two had been very close to each other, Wentworth and Jackson, though they were master and man.

"There isn't much more to it, sir," Jackson said slowly. "You were in pretty bad shape yourself, you'll remember. When you began to get better, I was well on the road to recovery also. It seemed like a good idea to surprise you, come back unexpected like."

Wentworth laughed grimly. "Very timely, your return," he said. "You saved my life in Penn Station—again. Saved Miss Nita at Macy's. I'm afraid the balance is in your favor now, Jackson. I'll have to do something to even the odds."

Jackson couldn't pull his eyes off the floor, and a slow red flood suffused his face. Nita, gripping Wentworth's arm with both hands, laughed softly.

Finally Jackson looked up. "The Lancia is in wretched condition, Major," he said formally. "If the Major will excuse me...."

Wentworth waved dismissal and sat very still, watching Jackson's broad shoulders retreat through the doorway with the least little swagger in their movement. He smiled. Nita sighed contentedly beside him.

"It's good to have him back..." she said.

Wentworth nodded. "I'll have to find another name for Jackson. It's possible our enemies might dig up that confession he made to being the Spider."

"Dick, you don't seem very much elated," Nita said slowly. "Jackson's back, the Fiddler's dead, and we can celebrate that dinner we planned tonight...."

Wentworth shook his head. "The Fiddler isn't dead," he insisted grimly. "And there'll be no safety in this city until he is captured. I'm hoping to smash him tonight before he can organize a new gang. Perhaps we can have a little midnight supper...."

His voice was heavy and dull. He was very tired. The evaporation of his elation left him strangely empty. He touched the back of his neck gingerly. The pain of Jerry Horace's blow made a dull aching through his head.

"Tonight, Nita," he said slowly.

HE SPENT the rest of the afternoon in reading newspaper accounts of the Macy's battle. At his request Flynn had made no mention of Wentworth's part in the warning and all credit had been given to one William Horace, first class patrolman put on special duty by Kirkpatrick. Printed in the paper was a facsimile of Kirkpatrick's bold handwriting ordering the search for the Death Fiddler. There were photographs of Bill and his mother.

But the best news Wentworth had was a telephone message from the hospital stating that Kirkpatrick had passed the crisis and was definitely on the mend. Wentworth was sure, too, that the panegyrics of the newspapers over the conquest of the Death Fiddler would definitely spell Kirkpatrick's election....

Yes, all the news was good, all of it except one thing—the city was satisfied that the Death Fiddler was captured but Wentworth knew he was still at large, knew that as long as that man lived, neither the city nor anyone in it was safe. As always, the ultimate battle depended upon the Spider. As always, he would go to that battle alone, with the lives of hundreds depending on his shrewdness, on the split-second precision of his planning....

When darkness had fallen, Wentworth retired to his room and very carefully assumed a new disguise. As he worked, he glanced frequently at a cabinet photograph before him, amending what he saw there with what he knew. When he stepped back, satisfied, there remained but one thing to be done. He stepped close again, and painted a bullet hole in the middle of his forehead.

It was a masterly job, that bullet hole, quite as good as the Fiddler had achieved in assuming the character of Dodson Larrimore. So good that afterward, when Wentworth sat down to a lonely supper, Jenkyns stared at him with horror in his eyes.

Wentworth seemed in no hurry. He dallied over coffee, barely sipped his liqueur. Later he began to pace the floor with long, nervous strides. At last the telephone buzzed faintly and he sprang to it, waving Jenkyns aside.

"All is ready, *sahib,*" came the voice at the other end.

Wentworth uttered an exclamation of delight. He caught up a hat which pulled well down over his brows and quickly left the building. His eyes were downcast and the operator of the elevator did not notice that this man had not the face of Wentworth.

Once outside, he strode swiftly down Fifth Avenue, turned a corner, and climbed into a rented Ford coupé parked at the spot. Minutes later, after weaving his way eastward and southward, he drew up before an apartment building which just escaped the tenement class. In the hall Jackson awaited him. Ram Singh had been busy on his face with make-up material and it no longer had the broad honesty that was natural to it.

No words passed between the two men as they climbed a flight of stairs and rang a doorbell.

From within came slow deliberate footsteps. The door opened wide. In the doorway, clothed in a cheap civilian suit stood Bill Horace.

"The Fiddler!" he gasped.

The cry was echoed within. Behind Horace, in the narrow hallway, appeared blonde Tony Musette, with Jerry by her side. On Jerry's face showed a mixture of pleasure and fear. There was no doubt about the girl's expression. She was frightened.

"Horace," Wentworth said to the policeman, and his voice was that of the Death Fiddler. "Horace, you destroyed my men. You wrecked my dreams. I have come to exact payment."

BILL HORACE tried to spring backward and slam the door, but Jackson was faster. Jackson went in with a blackjack in the palm of his hand. He struck once, then hauled the unconscious patrolman forward into the hall. Jerry's hand whipped to his gun, but Wentworth jerked the door shut on a steel rasp that would hold it tightly and, between them, he and Jackson carried Bill Horace to the first floor where they put him in a vacant apartment. Ram Singh bowed gravely in the half darkness created by the vagrant beams of a street light, and the unconscious policeman was given into his charge.

Wentworth rapidly removed his disguise and went back up the stairs. He had on a different hat and his topcoat had been discarded. The battering on the door of the apartment upstairs was thunderous put he managed to make himself heard above the shout.

"What's the matter?" he demanded.

A muffled banging on the door answered him, then a garble of voices. He slid a strip of steel down one side of the rasp, shouldered the door and shoved it in. Jerry Horace raced past him, gun in hand. Tony stood in the doorway and wrung her hands, while behind her stood an old woman with a quiet face. That would be Bill Horace's mother, Wentworth knew.

Wentworth caught Jerry by the shoulder and the boy slashed viciously at his hand with the revolver. A quick wrench captured the gun. Jerry Horace reeled pack, pale faced, against the wall, holding the arm which Wentworth knew Ram Singh's knife had pierced.

"What's the trouble?" Wentworth asked anxiously. "I came to pay Bill Horace a reward. I'd do a good deal to help him. Is there any trouble?"

"Give me that gun," Jerry snarled, moving forward on his toes.

Tony Musette caught at Wentworth's arm. "Please," she begged, "please save Bill. The Death Fiddler just came and took him away." Her fingers slipped from Wentworth's arm and she turned to Jerry. "Please, Jerry, save Bill. You know he's the one I love...."

Jerry stopped his advance and stared at her very steadily with his small dark eyes. "You love Bill?" He asked it almost softly.

Tony nodded her head miserably and Jerry drew a deep breath. "I knew it," he said bitterly. "I knew it all the time you were pretending I was the one...."

He whirled to Wentworth, who was looking in pretended amazement from one to the other. "Did you say," Wentworth asked incredulously, "that the Fiddler carried Bill Horace away?"

Jerry nodded impatiently. "Sure, nobody with any sense would have thought that Danny Dawson was the Fiddler. Listen, if you want to help me, give me that gun and let me go."

"I'll do better than that," Wentworth declared vehemently. "If you're going after the Fiddler, I'll go with you,"

He handed Jerry his revolver, caught his own heavy automatic from its holster. He balanced it for a moment on his palm, grinned crookedly at Jerry. "Lead on," he said.

Wentworth let Jerry call a taxi and he sat as tensely as Jerry on the edge of his seat while the cab sped up town under the black, thick pillars of the elevated.

"He ought to be here tonight," Jerry, said thickly. "He told us yesterday he would. He told me then that he didn't expect many of us would show up at the place today, but he'd be there just the same."

JERRY APPEARED to attach little significance to the words he pronounced, but Wentworth felt an almost uncontrollable jerking of his muscles. The Fiddler had told Jerry plainly, in the words the boy had just relayed, that the holdup of Macy's, as probably the Penn Station robbery, too, had been intended to wipe out the mob. And the Fiddler was waiting tonight to finish the job.

Wentworth knew that suddenly. He realized that the Fiddler would never have attempted such raids. The returns were too small in proportion to the risk. He realized, too, why Purviss had sent Larrimore to Macy's. Purviss had known the holdup would end in disaster, otherwise there would have been no point in sending Larrimore there.

"I don't think I'd go into this place recklessly," Wentworth told Jerry slowly. "I think if you do you'll walk into a stream of bullets."

Jerry said nothing. Wentworth was thinking that this was the man who had almost killed him earlier today, that he was a dangerous member of the Fiddler's mob, probably more trusted than most of the others. And all this dated back to the moment in the hall of the Tory hotel when the Fiddler had joined Jerry in protecting Tony from one of his underlings.

There was a white purity about Jerry's face as it was set now. The meanness and slyness had gone. This man was intent upon only one thing now, saving his brother for the girl they both loved.

The taxi whirled abruptly westward and pulled up before the only apartment house in the block. Jerry sprang out and dived for the doors. Wentworth tossed a bill to the driver and raced after his guide.

He was seconds too late. Jerry had sprung into the elevator, slammed the door and was shoving upward.

Wentworth stood cursing. If he ran up the stairs, he would not know at what floor to stop. He had to stand and wait until the automatic elevator stopped.

It checked at the fourth floor and Wentworth pulled the elevator back again by pressing the button by the side of the door. The cage descended with maddening slowness. With it finally at hand, Wentworth wrenched open the door, sprang inside, waited with enforced calm while the car sighed upward.

As he stepped into the hall, he heard a muffled shot and whirled toward the sound. Undoubtedly it came from behind the door at the end of the hall. Wentworth started toward it, then checked, remembering. Flinging toward the steps he crept on silent feet to the apartment above the one where he had heard the shot. He tried the door gently, brought a slender lockpick of surgical steel into play, slipped the bolt.

He flung the door wide, sprang inside with gun in hand. A man jumped upright behind a small table on which a microphone was placed. He snatched up a revolver from the table, but Wentworth's gun had already spoken. The shot took the man squarely between the eyes and spilled him backward over his chair to the floor. He did not stir.

Wentworth walked slowly over and stared down at the dead man. His lips twisted in a wry smile. There was no doubt that *this* man was the Death Fiddler. His pale face stared up at Wentworth, a duplicate of the one Wentworth himself had worn a short while ago, even to the bullet hole between the eyes. The dead man, the Death Fiddler was—*was Dodson Larrimore!*

EVERYTHING WAS clear now—even why Larrimore had been ordered to Macy's. He had ordered himself there to tip off the police and wipe out the mob which was becoming dangerous to its leader. Doubtless he already had accumulated more money than he could ever hope to use. The device of ordering himself killed by Limpy Magee was a neat trick to destroy suspicion against himself, and he had picked a man he had thought incapable of carrying the crime through—Limpy Magee.

Undoubtedly Larrimore had had a death-hold over the Mayor or his political superiors, and it was through them he had controlled prosecutor and courts. Wentworth remembered, with a startled sense of surprise, how Purviss often stood aside as if in deference to Larrimore, how in the Pennsylvania Station, he had aped Larrimore's explanation of his being knocked out, a story which was to help throw suspicion on Purviss himself.

Well, Larrimore—the Death Fiddler—was dead now. The battle over. Wentworth bent to the periscope which showed the room below—and his lips tightened. The false wax figure of the Fiddler was there. And even as he had feared, Jerry lay dead almost on the threshold. There could be no doubt of death because the bullet had torn away the side of his head.

Yet there was a strange peace on the dead face. He had come to bring back to the girl they both loved the brother whom the girl preferred. Wentworth suspected he did not find death unwelcome.

Wentworth straightened from the periscope, bent above the dead Fiddler and placed his scarlet death seal upon the forehead beside the bullet hole. It occurred to him ironically that the Spider, as Limpy Magee, had been ordered to kill Dodson Larrimore in precisely this way, on this very day. He stood erect and cast one quick glance about the barren room.

Distantly, a single silvery note gonged. Wentworth glanced down at his watch and soft, mocking laughter escaped from his lips.

It was eleven-thirty, Thursday night.